The Disappearing Duchess

THE
LAST APPRENTICE

The Disappearing Duchess

IMOGEN ROSSI

HOT
KEY
BOOKS

With special thanks to Rosie Best

First published in Great Britain in 2013 by Hot Key Books
Northburgh House, 10 Northburgh Street, London EC1V 0AT

Text copyright © Working Partners Limited 2013

The moral rights of the author have been asserted.

A CIP catalogue record for this book is available from the British Library.

ISBN: 978-1-4714-0183-1

1

Typeset by Palimpsest Book Production Limited, Falkirk, Stirlingshire
This book is typeset in 11pt Sabon LT Std

Printed and bound by Clays Ltd, St Ives Plc

FSC

Hot Key Books supports the Forest Stewardship Council (FSC),
the leading international forest certification organisation, and is committed
to printing only on Greenpeace-approved FSC-certified paper.

www.hotkeybooks.com

Hot Key Books is part of the Bonnier Publishing Group
www.bonnierpublishing.com

Chapter One

'Powdered sheep's bones, beetle shells, lead, clay, azurite, onion skins, pollen from flowers harvested at the full moon, and the mucus of a certain snail . . .'

Bianca just watched, her legs curled under her on the cool tiled floor as her master, the great Annunzio di Lombardi, strode around the Duchess Catriona's chambers listing the ingredients of paint pigments. The Duchess sat on a long couch, her red silk skirt gathered around her, sketching her view of the sun-baked courtyard through the white stone arches.

'. . . ground together by hand to release their natural acids. Bianca!' di Lombardi barked, turning so sharply, the end of his long white beard wrapped around his shoulder. 'Show the Duchess.'

Bianca scrambled to her knees and held up her metal tray. The glazed clay pots clinked together, filled with all the ingredients di Lombardi had named, and several more.

Di Lombardi's instructions had been very clear when he'd

chosen Bianca to assist him at the Duchess's art lessons. *Do not stare. Do not speak. Do not fidget and fiddle. In fact, if you can follow my orders without breathing, please do so.*

Bianca tried. But it was hard when the Duchess was only two years older than her with dark, dancing eyes and a wicked sense of humour.

'Beetle shells? And . . . mucus?' the Duchess repeated dubiously.

Bianca stifled a smile as Duchess Catriona swept a strand of red-gold hair from her face and leaned in to peer into the pots, her nose wrinkling. She had a birthmark on her cheek that Bianca had never seen before, because she was always painted without it. Bianca didn't know why; she thought it was quite becoming.

'Nothing wrong with mucus,' said di Lombardi. 'Art can come from anywhere, Your Highness.'

'The murex snail . . .' Bianca began, and then clamped her lips together.

Di Lombardi looked at her. 'Yes, Bianca, why don't you explain to us about the murex snail?' He gave her a tiny nod.

Di Lombardi had given her the same nod the first time she'd been allowed to help paint a few of the shadows in one of his magical trompe l'oeil scenes. Bianca remembered the flush of terror she'd felt as she'd raised her brush. He wouldn't have allowed her to do it if he hadn't believed she could. But still, she'd had to brace her elbow against the wall to keep her hand from shaking. Her heart beat almost as fast now.

She put down her tray and sat up straight to address the Duchess.

'Um, well. It's a very rare snail, and its mucus is purple, and you make amazing purple dyes from it. Most of the purple clothes we have are dyed with it, but it's very expensive, and hard to make, and that's why only very important people . . .' She met di Lombardi's fierce eyes and broke off, bowing her head.

Bianca swallowed. *I've done it now. I'm going to be washing out the sulphur pots this evening, for certain.*

'My gown for the Ascension is purple,' said Duchess Catriona, evenly. Then she giggled, the birthmark wrinkling with her smile. 'I can't wait to tell Baron da Russo that I'm wearing a snail-slime dress!'

Bianca had to disguise her own laugh with a cough.

'Very amusing, Your Highness,' said di Lombardi, his bushy eyebrows drawing together. 'My hilarious assistant will now demonstrate how we create paint with a carmine red.' He gave Bianca another nod.

Bianca straightened her back and scanned the clay pots in front of her, picking out the one filled with small dried insect shells. They glistened deep red-brown as she poured a handful into her mixing bowl.

Di Lombardi carried on talking and pacing, his shoes clacking across the white and ochre tiles while Bianca ground the shells into a fine, sticky powder with a stone pestle. The crushed shells brightened from reddish-brown into a vivid blood red. 'Of course, there are more complicated alchemical processes, which are far too dangerous and secret to perform outside my studio. Now, the green—'

'Are they magical paints, then?' the Duchess interrupted, her eyes bright with curiosity. Her skirts rustled as she shifted on the couch. 'I've always wondered whether your wonderful illusions were enchanted before or after the picture is finished.'

'With the greatest respect, Your Highness, that is not your concern,' said di Lombardi. For a moment Bianca thought he was annoyed, but he met her eye, and gave the tiniest hint of a wink. Then his face went back to its natural dour expression and he turned his back to her, addressing the Duchess. 'Now, this is very important: you must beware the green.'

Bianca couldn't help rolling her eyes. She knew this was a crucial lesson, but even though she was di Lombardi's youngest apprentice she felt like she'd heard him give it hundreds of times.

'*Green pigment is as dangerous as it is beautiful,*' she mouthed along with her master. '*For it is made with arsenic, and so it is very, very poisonous!*' Her words matched di Lombardi's exactly. He even used the same tone of voice every time, rising and falling dramatically. She opened her eyes wide like a mad soothsayer as di Lombardi worked up to the big finish, gesturing with his arms wide. A gesture Bianca copied. '*Beware the green! Or else, you could go mad, and then blind, and eventually die!*'

Bianca looked up to see what effect di Lombardi's speech had had on the Duchess, and nearly dropped her pestle.

The Duchess was staring at Bianca. She'd caught her mimicking her master. But instead of saying anything, the Duchess smiled at her, then fixed her attention on di Lombardi.

Bianca let out a long breath of relief.

'Now, Your Grace,' di Lombardi said to the Duchess, 'what must you do?'

'Beware the green, Master di Lombardi,' said Duchess Catriona, her face suddenly serious.

Di Lombardi nodded his approval and then spun around. 'Is that carmine ready yet, Bianca?'

'Er . . .' Bianca turned away hurriedly, working the pestle hard into the red powder. 'Nearly, Master.'

Di Lombardi stretched. His old bones creaked and cracked. 'Well, while Bianca's finishing her work, let me take a look at today's sketches.'

Duchess Catriona passed him her sheaves of parchment. Di Lombardi looked through them, his eyebrows twitching as he turned over each one.

'Hmm. Not bad,' he said.

The Duchess grinned. Not many people in the city of La Luminosa would dare to criticise their beloved Duchess, but 'not bad' was high praise from Annunzio di Lombardi.

'This shade study is well done. You've almost captured the brilliance of the sunlight on the marble, but . . .' He turned over another sheet and shook his head. 'No, no, no. Very poor perspective on this one. You see how this tree looks, in comparison to this fountain? Let me show you . . .' di Lombardi reached over to the low marble table beside the Duchess's couch, but his hand closed on thin air. 'Where's my chalk?'

Bianca looked around, but she couldn't see Master di Lombardi's chalk anywhere. He started stalking around the room, moving cushions, picking up the corners of rugs, and peering through the leaves of the potted orange trees. He tugged aside a curtain at one end of the room and glared into the antechamber beyond. A group of people looked back at him in confusion. They were barefoot, and dressed in simple coloured tights and tunics. One man was balancing on one hand, and two others were holding a woman up in the air in a flying pose.

'*Pfft*, players,' di Lombardi muttered, turning away.

Bianca glanced at the Duchess. She was gazing at the painted ceiling, watching the illusions of clouds and jewel-coloured birds fly overhead, her face pulled into an expression of total indifference. Bianca guessed this innocent look must mean the Duchess was guilty of something.

Master di Lombardi frowned in suspicion. 'Your Highness hasn't seen my chalk, I'm sure,' he said. Duchess Catriona's expression didn't change but her eyes flickered to the painted wall behind him.

The old man turned to look at the wall and huffed through his beard. The scene was one of his own trompe l'oeil paintings, magically enhanced like the ceiling. Although the wall was solid, a masonry archway had been turned into a living picture of a balcony overlooking softly rolling green hills. The leaves on the trees swayed in a breeze and the silhouettes of birds circled lazily in the

6

bright blue sky. Golden sunlight flooded into the room through the mural. Bianca could even feel the painted sun's heat gently warming her face whenever she walked by.

Di Lombardi sighed and sank creakily to his knees. He reached out and put his hand inside the painting, fishing around underneath a painted couch on the painted balcony. His arm vanished up to the elbow.

A few seconds later, the Duchess broke down and giggled as he pulled out a long stick of blue chalk. 'Come, Master di Lombardi, I'm sure I'm not the first of your pupils to get sick of the sight of that thing,' she laughed.

But you're certainly the first to let him know it! Bianca thought.

Di Lombardi simply raised one bushy eyebrow, and the Duchess fell dutifully silent. He started to correct her drawing with long, assured strokes of the chalk.

Bianca's attention was distracted by the soft thud of hands and feet on stone floor. The curtain to the anteroom had been left open, and she could just about see the players practising inside. She shifted her position for a better look.

A man and a woman were rehearsing a silent play, miming that they were trapped on different sides of an invisible wall. Next to them, another man wearing an enormous golden ruff was reciting words she couldn't hear from a script while making gestures with his arms. Two girls of about six hopped and skipped together, perfectly mirroring each other's movements.

Bianca gasped as a boy who looked about her own age crossed the room in a mad tumble of limbs. But then the boy straightened his arms and legs and transformed his roll into a graceful cartwheel, leaping into a mid-air somersault right at the end and landing with a flourish. Bianca had to clench her fists in her skirt to stop herself from applauding.

The boy relaxed, brushing the back of his hand across his cheek to push back his hair.

'Marco!' A man with a long painted stick waved the boy over. He gave him a gentle tap on the head with the orb on the end of the stick. 'If you do that during a performance you'll smudge your make-up. Remember, if you can be seen by the public, you are on stage! Try to act like it.'

Bianca smiled at the familiar tone. Did all masters speak to their apprentices like this?

The boy gave the man a sheepish grin. 'Yes, Father.'

'Do you like harlequin plays, Bianca?'

Bianca jumped and felt her face go as red as her carmine paint. Duchess Catriona had risen from her couch and now stood beside her, and she'd clearly noticed that Bianca was distracted from her work. But she didn't seem angry – she was smiling again.

'I've never seen one, Your Highness,' Bianca mumbled.

'Is that so?'

'Not a proper one, anyway,' Bianca continued. 'There are jugglers in the Piazza del Fiero sometimes, but they're nothing like these.'

The Duchess's eyes twinkled. Bianca was beginning to wonder why she'd been so terrified the first time they'd met.

'Master Xavier's players are practising for my Ascension festivities,' the Duchess said. 'I just love this particular troupe, they'll be a large part of the four days of celebrations. There'll be a harlequin show along with the ball tonight, tomorrow we're holding a masque, then the troupe perform a play on the third night, and they'll be there to entertain the crowd at my coronation too.' She turned to di Lombardi and clapped her hands. 'Master di Lombardi, you must bring Bianca to the celebration tonight! In fact, bring *all* your apprentices.'

'The apprentices have work to do, Your Highness,' di Lombardi said gruffly.

'Nonsense,' said the Duchess, dismissing him with a flap of her brightly coloured fan. 'I'm sure they deserve a break, and what better time than my birthday? I should declare it a national holiday. Perhaps that will be my first act as ruler. Well, after building my new Royal College.' A dreamy look crossed her face. 'I'm going to make La Luminosa the centre of the civilised world. People will come thousands of miles to learn to be artists and doctors and great thinkers . . .'

'There are some who say you should be looking for a husband, not indulging your own whims,' said di Lombardi drily.

Bianca held her breath, but the Duchess folded her hands in her lap and pursed her lips challengingly. 'You are not one of them, though, are you, Master?'

Di Lombardi's bushy eyebrows twitched and he said nothing.

'I will marry, of course,' she continued, 'but not for a few years. The Baron has been a good Regent,' she said, though her voice sounded a little flat, as if she were reciting from a playscript. 'But he's so *stuffy*. I'm going to make some real changes.'

'Not until you officially turn fourteen,' said di Lombardi. 'And that's not for four days.' He glanced out through the arches at the sun-drenched world outside. Bianca followed his gaze. Beyond the courtyard she could see down into the city where the sparkling ribbons of the canals wound between the buildings, busy with gondolas going about their business. Di Lombardi seemed to stare out at the Duchess's subjects for some time before he turned back into the room. 'Your Highness, I would speak with you privately before we finish your lesson.'

'Ah . . .' Duchess Catriona's smile dimmed slightly. 'Yes, of course.' She stood and followed him into another antechamber.

Bianca got up and started to pack away the lesson. She collected the Duchess's sketching papers and piled them up neatly on a side table, and made sure di Lombardi's special chalk was safe in its compartment in his brush bag. She was just stacking her own pots when she heard a loud rustle of silk. The Duchess was running back towards her, in a distinctly un-Duchess-like fashion. She held her ruby-red skirts up with both hands, and strands of her hair fell loose around her face. For a moment Bianca thought she looked just like one of the market girls who fetched and carried across the Piazza del Fiero.

'Here!' she whispered, thrusting a soft handkerchief into Bianca's paint-stained fingers. 'Come tonight. Show this to the guards and they'll let you in.' She gave a wide grin that wrinkled the freckly birthmark on her right cheek, then turned and dashed back to the antechamber.

Bianca unfolded the handkerchief and gasped at the intricate design embroidered on one corner in gold thread: a C for Catriona on top of the bright sun emblem of the city-state of La Luminosa. A royal invitation. Her head was spinning as she continued to pack away her things.

She was going to the Ascension Ball!

Chapter Two

As she crossed the bridge over the Grand Canal, Bianca hesitated, smoothing down her best dress. It was the only one she had that wasn't torn or covered in blotchy paint stains, but it was rather scratchy and uncomfortable – and *plain* compared to the glittering finery of all the people around her. A huge crowd streamed past, chattering and laughing, taking out their golden invitations ready to present them to the guards. Bianca swallowed and clutched the Duchess's handkerchief tightly as she joined the flow of people crossing the bridge. What if they still didn't let her in? What if they thought she'd stolen it?

She had barely felt worried at all when she'd been sneaking out of her bedroom in the attic of di Lombardi's studio. It had been easy, actually, pulling on her dress underneath her blanket, carefully stepping over the creaky floorboard to avoid waking her roommate Rosa, and creeping down the dark stairs past the servants' rooms.

Now she found herself gazing up at the palace. The

great white arched entrance blazed just like the sun that glimmered on its banners. Candles shone out of every window and crackling lamps lined the walls. The city of La Luminosa was a place of light and warmth even in the longest winter night, but tonight the palace gave off such brightness that the canal looked like a river of melted gold.

She stopped in front of a guard, and held out the handkerchief in a trembling hand.

'I, um, I haven't got an invitation,' she mumbled. 'But I have got this . . .'

The guard watched her unfold the handkerchief. Bianca felt foolish and prepared herself to be humiliated.

But to her relief, he gave her a courteous nod of his head then stepped aside, allowing her to enter.

'Thank you!' Bianca folded the handkerchief carefully and stuffed it back in her pocket. Walking past the guard, she had to suppress the urge to skip. Instead she tried to walk like a lady, with her nose in the air, looking the nobles in the eye. She had been officially invited, after all.

The palace courtyard was as bright as a piazza on a midsummer day, and just as crowded. Except, instead of street sellers hawking long strings of spiced meats and rolls of fabric and carved wooden pots, there were fire-jugglers and musicians all around the grand fountain and a group of people in ornate masks dancing a stately pavane.

Bianca stopped for a few minutes to watch the dance, entranced by the graceful sweep of the ladies' skirts and the bright rainbow colours of the men's coats, then followed the crowd inside. It felt very strange to be walking into

13

the palace with so many grand people. Would they guess she was a fraud?

Bianca found her way to the central ballroom where the Duchess would make her appearance. Her stomach rumbled at the sight of long tables laden with more food than she had ever seen in her life. She was just reaching out to take a glazed sugar ball from one of the tables when she heard someone cry out, 'Master di Lombardi, what an honour!'

She ducked behind a group of chattering ladies just in time as di Lombardi walked up to the table. He was trailed by a crowd of men and women, all open-mouthed with amazement at seeing the legendary artist in the flesh.

'Master di Lombardi, what is the secret of your magical paintings? I simply must know!'

'Master, I dabble in painting myself, if you'd like to see . . .'

'What can you tell us about the painting you're unveiling tonight? I hear it's simply divine . . .'

Di Lombardi grimaced at them. His balding head seemed to sink into the folds of his cloak, like a grumpy tortoise's, and he answered each question with a sombre grunt of disapproval. Di Lombardi didn't like people much at the best of times, but he detested praise, calling it 'empty-headed piffle'.

Bianca moved away, losing herself in the crowd. *He'll have me cleaning the brushes for a year if he sees me!*

Keeping to the back of the crowd, Bianca circled the room until she could get a good look at the main entertainment – the troupe of players. They were right in the middle of a harlequin show, tumbling and singing to each other. The harlequin character in his red and black diamond costume was tricking the silly Baron into freeing his slaves. Bianca stifled a loud laugh when she realised the actor playing the Baron was dressed in a flowing black cloak with a deep blue trim, just like the one the Baron da Russo usually wore. She looked around, and sure enough there was the real Baron, wearing the same cloak, and glaring at the players. His round, red face was even redder than usual.

When the show ended, the players bowed to the guests and tumbled out of the room. After only a few seconds they came back – their faces were still painted with bright shapes and colours, but they'd changed out of their elaborate costumes and into red breeches and coats, and they carried bottles and glasses of wine.

Master Xavier raised his painted stick and called out to the crowd. 'My Lords and Ladies, if you will join us in the salon, Master di Lombardi will now reveal his birthday commemoration of the Duchess Catriona.'

The crowd began to move, jostling to get into a good position to see the famous painter's latest masterpiece. Bianca jostled too – she'd never even seen the cartoons for this painting. Di Lombardi had done all the work himself, in some secret place not even the apprentices knew about.

A boy in red with a blue lightning streak down his face called out, 'Master di Lombardi!' and stepped into di

Lombardi's path holding a thick blue bottle and a wine glass. Then he stumbled and fell and the crowd around him gasped. Bianca threw her hands up, thinking he was going to drop the bottle and hurt himself on the broken glass . . . but he turned his fall into a graceful roll, keeping the bottle and glass unharmed, and presented them both to di Lombardi. The crowd applauded. Bianca saw the boy raise his hand to wipe at his face, then pull it back again, and she grinned.

'Your favourite, Sir, from the vineyards in the northern hills,' the boy said, pouring a glass for di Lombardi.

Di Lombardi dipped his head at the boy, but did not thank him. When he looked up from his bow he saw Bianca. His expression turned frosty and he glared at her.

Oops.

A nobleman in a Prussian-blue coat took di Lombardi's arm and steered him towards the salon, and he went with a last piercing glance back at Bianca. She sighed, mentally lining up the jobs she was going to be doing for the next ten years: cleaning dirty pots, crusted-up paintbrushes, the dusty floor covered in wood-shavings . . .

Still, now he knew she was there, there was no harm in watching the unveiling before she left, was there? There wasn't much chance that she'd be able to attend the masque or the play celebrating the Duchess's Ascension over the next three nights, so Bianca might as well get all the pleasure she could now.

Keeping a prudent distance from di Lombardi, she followed the crowd into the chamber where a huge canvas took up most of one wall of the room, covered by a velvet curtain. Bianca looked around, almost as excited to see Duchess Catriona's reaction to the painting as she was to see the painting itself.

'Ahem. Ladies and gentlemen,' growled di Lombardi, stifling a small cough. 'Due to unforeseen circumstances, the Duchess will not be joining us tonight.'

A groan of disappointment rippled through the crowd.

What a shame the Duchess couldn't come to her own party. I hope she's not unwell, thought Bianca. *She's due to be crowned in just three days.*

'Now,' said di Lombardi, silencing them with a raised hand, 'I have the greatest pleasure to present to you, my gift to Duchess Catriona on the occasion of Her Highness's fourteenth birthday . . .' he reached up and tugged on a golden tassled rope attached to the curtain.

The velvet fell away, and light flooded the room. Bianca's heart soared, and the crowd let out a sigh of appreciation. The painting was an almost lifesized picture of the room at the top of the White Tower, the Duchess's favourite room in the palace. Magical sunlight shone out from the canvas and lit up the real chamber and the stunned faces of the guests. The marble floor gleamed, beautiful textured tapestries hung on the wall, an inviting-looking cream-coloured couch sat under the wide windows, birds circled in the sky outside, and you could see the stunning view of La Luminosa far below.

'Dear di Lombardi,' said a voice. 'I certainly would not miss this.'

Duchess Catriona stood at the back of the room with Baron da Russo, a wide smile on her face. The crowd sighed with pleasure and dipped their heads at the sight of their Duchess.

Di Lombardi gasped, too, and choked on his wine. He looked from the painting to the Duchess, and carried on coughing. The glass of wine tumbled from his hand as he clutched at his throat and chest.

'Master? Master!' Bianca tried to push through the crowd to di Lombardi's side. Through the shifting gaps between the guests, she saw him drop to his knees, then collapse flat onto the floor. The crowd gasped and muttered, someone shouted for help. A lady stepped on Bianca's foot and a young man accidentally elbowed her in the nose, but she managed to squeeze between them to kneel beside her master.

'Fetch a doctor!' she cried.

Master di Lombardi choked again, and looked up at her. The flesh around his eyes was puffy and swollen. His gaze fixed on her and his mouth opened. She had to lean down, her hair trailing on the floor, to hear what he was trying to say.

'Duchess . . .'

Bianca looked up, about to fetch the Duchess, but she felt di Lombardi's wrinkled fingers close around her hand. He pressed something long and thin into her palm. She knew what it was from the touch alone: a paintbrush.

Di Lombardi coughed once more and his fingers tightened on Bianca's wrist as he pulled her even closer. 'Hidden . . .

rooms, secret passages . . . second city . . .' he whispered. 'Protect . . . the Duchess . . .'

'What?' she asked.

But di Lombardi's eyes rolled back until there was just a sliver of white between his swollen eyelids, and then his grip loosened and he fell back, unconscious.

'Master!' she cried.

Chapter Three

'Make room, girl,' said a man swooping down to di Lombardi's side like a crow in a sweep of black cloak. The doctor put his fingers to di Lombardi's throat, pushed apart his eyelids and pulled out his tongue. Bianca stood by, twisting her hands in her skirt, hardly able to breathe.

'He is alive,' said the doctor finally. Bianca let out a sigh of relief. 'He's had an attack of apoplexy. We must get him to his home immediately so I can treat him.' He signalled to a servant who was standing nearby. 'Clear this room at once!' he shouted. The crowds slowly drifted away. 'And fetch a cart and stretcher.' The servant hurried off.

'Will he wake up, doctor?' Bianca asked.

The doctor got to his feet and brushed down his black robe, avoiding Bianca's eyes. 'He may,' he said.

Misery rose in Bianca's throat. '*He may*' could just as well mean '*he may not*'.

'Are you one of his apprentices?'

Bianca nodded.

'Then you'd better run back and rouse the household.'

The doctor waved over a couple of servants who were hovering in the doorway with a long stretcher. The doctor helped lift di Lombardi gently and herded the servants out, leaving Bianca alone in the room.

She glanced up at the beautiful painting, still casting its magical golden light over the floorboards.

Could this be my master's final work?

The now empty room blurred and glimmered in front of her and she shook her head fiercely and wiped her eyes on her sleeve.

She had to be practical, she had to tell the others what had happened. She backed off, her knees trembling, and almost tripped over something on the floor. It was a small dog, a little white thing that must belong to one of the noble guests, judging by its jewel-studded collar and neat, clean fur.

The dog yipped at her, and then put its head down and lapped at a deep red puddle of wine that had spilled onto the floor. Her master's favourite wine, brought to him specially –

Suddenly, the little dog choked. Its claws scraped the floor as it skidded backwards, away from the wine, its whole body shaking. It was choking like a cat with a hairball.

. . . just like Master di Lombardi.

Bianca felt the back of her neck prickle. Could di Lombardi have been . . . *poisoned*?

'Where is that wine bottle?' She spun on the spot, looking

all around the chamber, but she couldn't see it. Who'd had it last – di Lombardi, or the player who'd served him? She hoped she'd be able to recognise the boy without his make-up on. Where would they take a bottle of wine when it wasn't needed any more?

There was no time to lose. She hitched up her skirts and ran to the kitchen, nearly knocking down a group of straggling party guests who were lingering in the hall, gossiping in low voices.

The cook looked up in annoyance as she clattered down the long stairs and into the warm, copper-coloured kitchen.

'What are you doing here, girl? What is going on?' he folded his arms crossly, holding an intimidatingly large cleaver. 'I've been told the feast is cancelled – just what am I supposed to do with these stuffed swans? Feed them to the cat?'

Bianca shook her head. 'I'm sorry, I don't know. My master's been taken ill. I need to know what happens to the wine bottles when they come back from the ball.'

The cook glared at Bianca, but sighed and waved his cleaver towards a shelf where open bottles were bunched together – some half-full, some empty – ready to be washed. 'Over there.'

Bianca skidded across the warm tiles to the sink. The shelf was crowded with bottles in shades of green and brown and red glass, but none of those were the one she wanted – she was sure that the bottle had been blue. So where was it?

'Oh.' She let out a soft sigh of disappointment. One

22

bottle sat in the sink, already washed, ready to be re-used: the blue bottle with the label from the Northern Vineyards.

It was sparklingly clean.

Her shoulders sagged. The fact that it was the only bottle to have been cleaned was suspicious, but not hard evidence. She thanked the cook before heading out of the castle as quickly as she could. She had to get a move on if she was going to get the household ready before di Lombardi and the doctor arrived on the cart.

Pulling off her best shoes, Bianca ran barefoot through the streets and over the canals of La Luminosa to the tall house that was di Lombardi's studio, and her home. She let herself in through the back door to find Angela, the kitchen girl, snoozing in her chair by the fire, her hands smudged with soot. Bianca shook her by the shoulders.

'What? What's going on?' Angela's gaze focused on Bianca. 'It's the middle of the night, what are you doing up? And dressed like that?' Her mouth fell open. 'Did you sneak –?'

'Angela, Master di Lombardi's been taken ill!'

Angela sat bolt upright. 'Is he all right?'

'No. He's . . . he won't wake up.'

Angela looked stricken for a second, then stood and wiped her hands down on her smock.

'I'll wake Mistress Quinta. She'll know what to do.'

Somehow, Bianca doubted it.

A few minutes later, the freshly awakened apprentices gathered in the studio by the light of a few candles. Sebastiano sat on the model's stool, staring at his knees. Rosa wandered

23

in a circle touching the palettes and brushes, as if she wanted to hold on to something normal. Domenico chewed his fingernails. Bianca felt very small, even though the others were only a few years older than her. They all kept giving her kind, worried glances.

Cosimo, the head apprentice, held Bianca at arm's length, frowning sternly. 'How dare you disobey Master di Lombardi's orders? You are in so much trouble. Don't think this tragedy is going to get you out of it.'

'No, Cosimo,' Bianca said meekly.

Cosimo's face softened and he gathered Bianca into a brief hug. Then he turned to the other apprentices. 'Master di Lombardi will be fine,' he said, just as if by giving orders and saying something could make it happen.

'What's wrong with him?' Sebastiano asked, without looking up from his knees.

'Well the doctor said it was apoplexy, but . . .' Bianca hesitated. The other apprentices looked up at her expectantly.

'But?' asked Rosa.

'But what, Bianca?' asked Cosimo.

'I think . . .' Bianca cleared her throat. It sounded pretty far-fetched now. 'Maybe there was something . . . something in the –'

There was a clatter of horses' hooves outside and the sound of the front door slamming open. Adults' voices, all talking over one another echoed down the hall.

'The doctor!' Bianca started forward, but the studio door opened and a man stepped inside and closed it behind

24

him. He was tall and dark-haired, with an angular face, and wore a jerkin and cloak of black embroidered with gold. His bright blue eyes swept over the studio, not quite focusing on the apprentices at first.

'Master Filpepi,' said Cosimo. He bowed, and gestured sharply for the others to join him. Bianca gave a clumsy curtsey, feeling her face go a little red. Piero Filpepi was the second best painter in the city, second only to di Lombardi. He'd been di Lombardi's apprentice himself, and now he had his own studio, and his own apprentices. Normally Bianca's heart skipped a beat when she thought about one day being just like him – though right now she felt like her heart hadn't been beating regularly for hours.

Filpepi's gaze landed on her, and then flitted off again. 'I had to come, when I heard what had happened. How are you all?'

'Is he here?' Bianca blurted out.

'Yes, I arrived just as the doctor's cart did. He's being taken upstairs via the front doors. Mistress Quinta will arrange everything, don't worry.' Filpepi looked around at the studio again, scanning the half-finished paintings and sculptures, the neat piles of sketches and cartoons. 'His work will need to be taken care of too. That's why I'm here. Master di Lombardi's commissions will be transported to my studio and finished there.'

What about us? Bianca could feel the question vibrating around the room, though none of the apprentices dared ask it, not even Cosimo. Without the commissions to work on, without their apprenticeships, they would be homeless.

of the apprentices had families they could return to, ...anca had no one.

Bianca's throat tightened. She'd lived here her whole life, ever since she was left on di Lombardi's doorstep as an orphaned child. Di Lombardi had taken her in, and had never spoken a word to make her feel as if she didn't belong here.

Filpepi was speaking again. 'We might as well take what we can carry back with us to my studio now.'

'. . . us?' Cosimo asked.

'Of course.' Filpepi's eyes widened. 'Oh, you poor things – I wouldn't abandon my dear friend Annunzio's apprentices at a time like this. You'll come and stay with me until – God willing – Annunzio makes a full recovery.' Bianca's heart leapt. She wished she could give Filpepi a hug. 'The truth is, I'll have twice the work to do now, so I'll need twice the assistance.'

The apprentices looked at one another, sharing smiles of relief.

'Hurry and collect your things,' Filpepi ordered.

Bianca scrambled with the rest, passing Cosimo the pile of sketches and heading back to her room to pick up her other dress.

But as she passed di Lombardi's room, she stopped and peered in. The servants were laying di Lombardi on his bed, stripping him of his boots and loosening his clothing. Mistress Quinta elbowed them aside, snapping, 'For God's sake, don't manhandle him like that, let me attend him.' Angela stood in the corner of the room, watching with tears in her eyes as the doctor and Mistress Quinta arranged the pillows and blankets, making her master comfortable. He was completely still, and his skin looked white and stretched over his bones like canvas. Angela looked at Bianca, shook her head, and then looked away.

Master Filpepi's offer was so generous, and she certainly couldn't turn him down to sit by her master's bedside when there was work to be done. But Bianca gathered her things with a heart as heavy as lead. How could she leave when someone might be trying to kill her master, and she was the only one who knew it?

Chapter Four

Filpepi's cart rumbled down the steep cobbled streets and over the wide bridges of La Luminosa. Bianca clutched a sheaf of sketches to her chest and gazed down into the sparkling waters of the Grand Canal. The bright moon danced and wavered in the water between the reflections of the sun-lamps that lined the bank.

'Here we are,' said Filpepi softly. 'Home.'

Bianca's stomach turned as she looked up. The large house in front of them was three times as big as di Lombardi's, set back from the street behind a lovely orchard-garden full of orange trees. Amber lanterns hung from their branches like glowing fruit.

But it wasn't home. In truth, Bianca wasn't sure she'd ever felt she was *home*: not even in the tall, crowded house in the centre of the city, with the creaking floorboards and the noisy neighbours, where Master di Lombardi now lay, barely clinging on to life.

She put her hand in her pocket and closed her fingers

lightly on the smooth wooden paintbrush di Lombardi had given her.

'Your house is very impressive, Sir,' said Cosimo.

Bianca rolled her eyes, but resisted the urge to kick him for being a suck-up at a time like this.

'Thank you, Cosimo,' said Filpepi. 'I'm so busy, I hardly have time to enjoy it.'

Of course Filpepi was busy. He took on all the commissions from people who'd like a di Lombardi painting, but couldn't afford one. And even though Filpepi wasn't as good a painter as di Lombardi, he'd always been better friends with Baron da Russo than Bianca's Master had. So while Master di Lombardi made time to tutor the Duchess and she commissioned plenty of paintings from him, all of the paintings the Baron had commissioned while he was Regent had come from Filpepi's studio. Filpepi was doing very well from the arrangement, or so Bianca had heard.

A bleary-eyed servant dressed in black and white opened the door of Filpepi's house as the cart came to a halt. The apprentices stumbled down, clutching the things they'd managed to bring with them. It wasn't much. Filpepi had told them to bring as many of their master's books and sketches as they could carry, as well as most of the paintings in progress, so Bianca and Sebastiano were loaded down with piles of paper. Rosa had a cloth bag that had her and Bianca's clothes bundled carelessly into it, and Domenico had one just the same for the boys. Cosimo was supervising the stack of canvases as they were carefully unloaded by the servants and carried inside. Everything else had been left behind.

Bianca and the others followed Filpepi through the door, through a large, echoey hall with a wide staircase and black and white ceramic tiles in a spiral pattern on the floor, and into his studio.

Bianca gazed around, impressed. It was just as grand as the rest of the house. Instead of worn wood and stone like in di Lombardi's studio, the counter tops were made of marble and polished slate. She hoped Filpepi's apprentices would tell her where everything was, or else she'd spend half her time searching for a brush in all the cupboards that lined the room.

'Why don't you take that side for Master Annunzio's work,' Filpepi said, gesturing to the left side of the room. 'Just move those paintings and that sculpture over here. Let's make sure we don't get our work mixed up, eh?'

Cosimo and the others hurried to obey, lifting unfinished works from their easels and placing di Lombardi's paintings there instead. Bianca and Sebastiano piled their armfuls of papers on the counter.

'Master?'

Bianca turned to see a young woman about Cosimo's age standing in the doorway. Four other young people stood behind her. They all looked sleepy with messy hair and ruffled clothes, and one of the boys yawned.

'Ah, Lucia, come in, come in,' Filpepi waved them into the studio. 'These are Master Annunzio's apprentices.'

Filpepi turned back to Bianca and the others. 'And these are my apprentices.'

Filpepi's apprentices didn't do much to hide their shock.

'They will be joining you in my studio until Master Annunzio is well again. Please make them welcome, look after them and show them to the dormitories. Lucia, the studio is going to be a little full, do make sure everyone has somewhere to work and that there's no confusion, won't you?'

'Of course, Master,' said Lucia. She walked up to Cosimo and gave him a short bow and a slight, supercilious smile. Bianca recognised the gesture – one head apprentice to another.

'I'll leave you to introduce yourselves,' said Filpepi, 'and see you in the morning.' He bowed out of the room, leaving the two groups of apprentices eyeing each other awkwardly.

Bianca met the eyes of the closest girl, who looked a little younger than she was, with a bob of messy brown hair that curled around her ears. She tried to smile apologetically, as if to say sorry for getting them all out of bed at a time like this. The girl did not smile back.

'This is Gennaro,' said Lucia, gesturing to the boy who'd yawned, 'Ezio, Francesca and Gabriella.'

'I'm Cosimo, Master di Lombardi's head apprentice,' said Cosimo. 'And this is Rosa, Sebastiano, Domenico and Bianca.'

'It's nice of you all to get up to greet us,' Rosa said.

The girl called Gabriella pushed her thick blonde curls out of her eyes and pulled a face. 'We didn't have the choice,' she said.

'Oh. Um – sorry,' Rosa muttered.

'We are all very sorry for your master,' said Lucia, through gritted teeth, with a glare at the other Filpepi apprentices. They shrugged and shuffled their feet.

'Yeah, sorry.'

'Sorry.'

'Thank you,' said Cosimo. He managed to sound grateful, as if their condolences had been genuine, but Bianca felt a flush of anger rise in her throat. Didn't they know her master was lying ill, maybe dying? Even if they weren't sympathetic, didn't they care that the city might lose the greatest artist who'd ever lived?

Lucia led them all upstairs and they split into boys and girls, the boys turning left and the girls going right. Lucia ushered the girls into a dorm room with two bunkbeds on one wall, a wardrobe, a small chest of drawers with a few pots of rouge and skin cream on top, and a plain mattress on the floor. The night lamp on its gleaming copper stand lit the room with a soft, golden glow.

'Gabriella, help Francesca make up your bed for Bianca,' Lucia ordered. 'You can take the mattress.'

Gabriella gave Lucia a look that could have singed her eyebrows off, but turned and helped Francesca, the youngest apprentice, to adjust the sheets on the bottom bunk.

'You'll be bunking with me,' Lucia told Rosa. She looked down at the sack. 'When will you fetch the rest of your clothes?'

'These are all my clothes,' said Rosa, coolly. 'And Bianca's, too.'

'Oh,' said Lucia. 'That's good – we won't have to clear out more than one drawer.' She pulled out the top drawer of the chest and carefully took out a handful of neatly paired stockings.

'Bianca, help me fold these,' Rosa said.

Bianca tried not to roll her eyes as she joined her, putting their clothes away neatly in the drawer – far more neatly than they usually did at di Lombardi's.

'Oh, I shouldn't bother. I'm sure you won't be here long,' said Lucia.

Bianca smiled at her. 'I'm sure you're right,' she said politely. 'Master di Lombardi will recover soon and we'll be out of your hair.'

Lucia paused, for just a little too long. 'Yes, of course, that's what I meant.'

Rosa grabbed Bianca's wrist just as she was about to turn and snap at Lucia. Rosa shook her head just a little, and Bianca sighed. She supposed they did have to be polite to Filpepi's apprentices. Still . . .

'Finished,' Gabriella sang, and came over to the chest of drawers. 'Have you?' She slapped her hand down on the top of the drawers. The pot of rouge wobbled and tipped up. Bianca reached for it, but she was too late – it fell into the drawer, spilling pink powder all over Rosa's best dress.

33

'Oh no,' said Gabriella, with a smug look right at Rosa. 'What a shame. At least it's only your old work clothes, right?'

Rosa's face darkened. 'Master Filpepi's been so nice to us. Why can't you be?' Gabriella snorted and opened her mouth to reply, but then the door opened and Cosimo put his head inside.

'It's very noisy in here!' he growled.

'Sorry, Cosimo,' said Rosa. 'We're just – it's fine. We're going to bed.'

Cosimo gave them all a worried glance and shut the door again.

'*Ooh Cosimo, sorry Cosimo,*' Gabriella sneered under her breath.

Rosa spun around, and for a second Bianca was afraid that she might actually hit her. But at last, Lucia intervened, grabbing Gabriella's shoulders and steering her away quickly.

Francesca spoke up. 'I'm sure everyone's tired. Everything will be much better in the morning.'

Bianca gave Francesca a grateful smile. Maybe at least one of them would be a friend.

Bianca changed into her nightgown quickly and got into bed below Francesca. She slid her feet under the covers – but they only got halfway down the bed, and abruptly caught on a tightly tucked sheet.

'What –?' Bianca wriggled and struggled, but no matter what she did, the sheets wouldn't budge. She got out of bed and pulled back the covers to see that Gabriella and

34

Francesca had folded her sheet in half before tucking it in.

She felt her face go red, but she wouldn't give them the satisfaction of reacting. She'd just fix it herself. She yanked the cover and sheet off the bed and started to tuck them back in properly.

Then she heard a sound from the top bunk. Francesca was giggling.

Bianca threw everything down on to the bed and turned around.

'Why are you being so mean?' she said. Gabriella and Lucia were both in bed, with their faces turned away. Neither of them answered. 'Why don't you care that our master is sick? We could all be homeless if Master di Lombardi doesn't get better!' She tried to keep her voice clear and calm, to shame them with the stupidity of it, but when they still ignored her, Bianca felt hot tears stinging the back of her throat. 'You're apprentices too, you're just like us!'

'Not quite as stuck up though,' came a muffled whisper from Gabriella's mattress.

'*Stuck up*? You don't know us!' Bianca's voice cracked and she folded her arms furiously. 'You're just jealous that our master is a better artist than Filpepi! Well, Filpepi has been kind to us. But if you can't do the same, then just – just leave us alone!'

She threw herself into bed and curled up, her arms wrapped tightly around herself. She wasn't going to cry. She didn't care what these girls thought of her.

The night lantern cast soft beams of light across the room. Bianca stared at the pattern, her vision slowly blurring and swimming with tears, despite herself. She listened to the soft, easy breathing of the other apprentices and wished again on every star in the bright night sky that her master would breathe easily again soon.

Chapter Five

The next morning, the two sets of apprentices gathered on either side of Filpepi's studio, like warring garrisons.

'Where's the commission for Madame de la Androzani?' asked Rosa, as she spun around, searching for the canvas. The easel she'd put it on the previous night was occupied by a painting of an Arabic man reclining in a lavishly decorated tent, surrounded by flowers and fruits.

'I don't know,' shrugged Gennaro. 'That's the easel we're using for the Sultan's painting.'

Cosimo sighed and affected a pleasant tone of voice, but Bianca could see his teeth were gritted. 'Master Filpepi told us to put it here,' Cosimo said. 'He gave us this side of the room.'

'Well, you can't have this spot,' Gennaro said. 'We need the light.'

'You're not even working on it! And your master –' Dominico began.

'*Your* master too,' Gennaro corrected him. 'For now.

And I don't think he did. The Sultan is far more important than some old woman.'

'Why don't you sort out your master's papers before you actually start touching anything?' Lucia suggested, with a patronising sneer.

Cosimo bristled, but then nodded. 'All right. Let's make sure we know where all our work is, shall we? Francesca, can you pass me those cartoons by your elbow?'

Bianca saw Francesca give Gabriella a swift glance before saying, 'No, I'm far too busy, do it yourself.'

Cosimo gaped at her. 'How dare –' He broke off. 'Bianca, collect the papers and sort them. All of them. Quickly!' he snapped.

Bianca fumed as she collected the papers together. She didn't want to be doing this. Should she tell him her suspicions? That someone wanted their beloved master to die, enough to poison his wine. But she just couldn't bring herself to do it. It sounded so far-fetched in the bright light of day. 'Yes, Cosimo,' she said meekly.

Madame di Androzani's portrait was located where it had been tossed against the far wall, and Sebastiano found a couple of spare easels that wobbled when you painted on them, but they were better than nothing.

'Can I help on a painting, Cosimo?' Bianca asked, when she'd done what he'd asked.

'No, we don't have enough space,' said Cosimo, with a swift glare at Lucia's back. 'Why don't you stick to setting out the paints for now, make sure we have everything we need?'

Bianca was careful not to roll her eyes until she'd turned away. She didn't think he'd appreciate being cheeked right now.

The apprentices set to work, and for a few moments there were no more arguments.

'Aren't you going to add any movement to that cat?' Lucia said. She was looming over Domenico's shoulder, her arms folded, as he painted a small study of a ginger cat sunning itself on the street.

'I – I don't know how to do that,' Domenico stammered. Lucia looked theatrically shocked.

'You don't know how to paint a moving cat? Not even a *respirare* so it looks like it's breathing, nothing? I thought you were all students of the great Annunzio di Lombardi! What has he been teaching you, if not that?'

Domenico gave Cosimo a pained glance. 'He – he says we need to learn how to paint without it first, so, so we understand what we're doing . . .'

'He says the painting and the artist both need to be properly prepared before magic gets involved,' Rosa said. Domenico looked pathetically grateful for her coming to his rescue, but Lucia just snorted and raised an eyebrow.

'Yes,' she said, with a patronising smile and another glance at his perfectly good cat painting. 'I suppose I can see why he'd think you aren't ready.'

Bianca flushed, embarrassed for Domenico – and a little for herself. She knew that the others were aware that di Lombardi had been letting her do a little bit of work on the magic paintings. They said they didn't mind. But still, she squirmed on the inside as she thought of the techniques she'd been learning, ones that even Cosimo hadn't mastered. Perhaps Filpepi's apprentices were better qualified than they were.

She looked over at the painting Lucia was working on, and frowned. That wasn't how you painted a *respirare*! Yes, the horse's sides were swelling and deflating, but it didn't look right at all. She obviously wasn't thinking about the animal's muscles, let alone where its bones were. How could Filpepi let his apprentices paint with magic without making sure they knew how to *paint*?

Bianca turned away, fed up. It would be practically suicide to point out Lucia's errors right now. But what good was she, standing here knowing how to create just as well as any of the others, but not allowed to help with any of di Lombardi's paintings?

Her eyes fell on the painting of the Sultan with his fruit and flowers. Nobody was working on that one, even though it was still taking up space on its easel, right in the good light. All of the apprentices were trying to ignore each other now, so nobody took much notice of her as she went over to it.

The bowls of fruit needed work. She could do that. She'd be able to make them look good enough to eat. She opened a pot of magical *shimmer* and a bright purple, and chewed her tongue in concentration. If she added colour and light to this bowl full of round, shiny grapes, in just the right way, she could make them *almost* look like the solid objects her master could paint into existence.

She raised her brush and began to work. It was detail, but Bianca knew that in a painting like this, the details could be everything . . .

'Hey, you! Girl! Stop!' Lucia's voice rang out, and a hand snatched the paintbrush out of Bianca's grip. 'How dare you?' Lucia yelled. 'This isn't one of your master's paintings! Didn't you hear me before, this is a portrait for the Sultan of Raj! How could you touch it? You could ruin it, do you want Master Filpepi to be humiliated?'

'I was just –'

'You obviously can't be trusted to be left unsupervised,' Lucia finished, and folded her arms. 'You can sit as a model for Gabriella's portrait instead.'

'But I was –' Bianca was about to tell her to look at what she'd done, that with just a few strokes she had improved it marvellously.

'Do not talk back to me, girl!' Lucia snapped.

'My name is Bianca!' Bianca yelled. Everyone turned to look at her. 'I've painted for the Duchess, and I *can* make a *respirare*, and I can make an *ether* wash, and I know a horse has ribs in its chest . . .'

'*Bianca!*' Cosimo hissed. 'Be quiet, right now. Go and sit for Gabriella's painting.'

'But Cosimo, they –'

'Now,' Cosimo growled.

Bianca cast Lucia a furious look.

Gabriella stepped in. 'Come over here,' she said. She went over to a door and opened it. On the other side Bianca

41

saw a big room full of all sorts of clothes – ballgowns and fur cloaks, britches and slashed doublets and guard uniforms. Gabriella came back with a huge, swishy skirt covered in bells and sequins, a collection of brightly coloured belts, and a shirt that ruffled stupidly around the neck. 'I'm painting the Duke of Rezia's daughter in their local traditional costume,' Gabriella said.

'I bet she's never worn this in her life,' Bianca muttered, as Gabriella wrapped the skirt around her, bound her up in the coloured belts and arranged the ruffles around her face. She caught Gabriella smirking, just for a second, before she told Bianca to shut up and sit still.

Bianca loathed modelling. Master di Lombardi had banned her from sitting for him years ago, after she'd fidgeted so much he'd almost given the child Santa Antonia three hands. Trying to sit still now, drowning in silly belts and ruffles while Lucia and Gabriella got to work on real paintings, was torture.

Lucia's horse wasn't getting any better, and she could see what Ezio and Francesca were doing.

Bianca winced as Ezio had to paint three layers of *shimmer* onto a window to make it reflect, but it looked more like water than glass. Someone obviously hadn't mixed the paint right. She wriggled on her stool in frustration and Gabriella yelled at her to sit still.

Francesca was painting a ray of light onto the background of a painting. Figures had already been painted in, probably by Filpepi himself – a group of people bowing to a tall, regally dressed woman – and Francesca wasn't letting her

42

brush get anywhere near the figures, clearly afraid that she couldn't paint neatly around them. Just how new was she?

Then Francesca's paintbrush slipped, trailing a long line of silvery paint down across background, in totally the wrong direction, as if the light had just decided to stop mid-air and go exploring. Bianca dug her fingernails into the stool in annoyance. If she was that girl's tutor, she'd have a few choice words for her . . .

But then Francesca threw her hands up over her mouth, still holding the paintbrush and getting a big blotch of paint in her hair. Her shoulders shook and she glanced at Lucia, who was busy trying to fix her horse, and Bianca saw her eyes were wet with tears. Despite her anger, Bianca felt a pang for Francesca. She knew what it was like to have a mistake to fix.

'Luncheon is ready,' called a voice. Bianca looked up. One of the cooks had stuck her head in through the studio door. Filpepi's apprentices immediately put down their brushes and headed out, trailed by di Lombardi's. Bianca saw Francesca visibly sag with relief.

She got down off the stool and walked over to her.

'Francesca,' she said, quietly.

Francesca jumped in the air and let out a little yelp, then saw Bianca and scowled. 'What? What do you want?'

Bianca suppressed the urge to just say something mean and walk away. 'I saw your mistake.'

'Oh.' Francesca's lip wobbled.

'It's OK,' said Bianca. 'I'm not going to tell on you. I can

43

fix it. The trick is not to let it dry. Where do you keep the paint remover?'

Francesca gave her a sideways look, as if she wasn't sure whether to trust her. But eventually she reached into a drawer underneath the nearest marble countertop and pulled out a large pot. 'But it won't work,' she said miserably. 'It's not strong enough.'

'Let's have a look.' Bianca unscrewed the lid. She dipped a clean sponge into the paint remover and sniffed it. 'Oh. Hmm.' She swiped at the bendy sunbeam. The paint remover barely smudged the surface. 'You're right. It's useless.' She threw down the sponge. 'Do you know where they keep the pure paint remover mixture, before they put water in it?'

'Um,' Francesca's eyes went wide. 'Well, yes um, it's up in that cupboard – but I'm not allowed –'

Bianca seized her stool and drew it up to the high cupboard. Inside there was a larger, heavier pot. She prized the lid off. The smell of *ether* and orange essence made her eyes water.

'That's better!' said Bianca as she climbed down from the stool. 'Now look, take just a little bit of the pure stuff –' she dipped a cloth into the mixture, '– like this, and start from the edges, and just work the mistake back into the part you were trying to paint. See?' she nudged at the edges of the meandering silver line until it vanished back into the background.

'That's amazing!' Francesca grinned. Bianca smiled back, and then picked up the paintbrush and the silver paint.

44

'Now, look, if you keep being as tentative as that you'll never learn to do this well.' She painted as she talked, using smooth, assured strokes to draw a straight line of light down towards the heads of the crowd and around the lady's outstretched hand, dabbing carefully to mark the different lengths of her fingers. 'It's much better to keep a good line and go over a little. You just need to practise!'

'Francesca?'

Bianca hid the paintbrush behind her back as Lucia walked in.

'Why aren't you at luncheon?' she said, as she marched back into the studio and planted her hands on her hips. 'You know Miss Lotti won't let you have any if you miss it.' Her eyes narrowed suspiciously. 'What are you two doing? Oh, Francesca, you haven't made *another* mistake, have you?'

Bianca shoved the paintbrush into Francesca's hand, hid the paint remover can under a dust sheet and turned away, peeling off the traditional costume.

'Lucia, I didn't –'

'I don't want to hear it, Francesca. I've told you before, you can't keep doing this, you know I don't want to have to tell Master Filpepi, but you can't stay in this apprenticeship if you –' She came around the easel and stopped with her mouth open. 'Oh!' Her mouth flapped open and closed as she searched for words. 'Oh. Well, this is a surprise! This is very good, Francesca. It's so neat . . .'

Bianca glanced up and met Francesca's eyes. Francesca swallowed.

'Um . . . actually, no Lucia, I –'

'She was helping me,' Bianca said quickly. 'I saw how neat she was being and asked for some tips.'

'Well, that's very kind of you, Francesca. To help the *least experienced* apprentices.' A sneering smile crossed Lucia's face. 'You should both get along to luncheon while there's still some left. Go on.'

Bianca and Francesca walked out of the studio together and down the hall.

'Bianca?' Francesca said quietly. 'I'm sorry . . .' she took Bianca's hand, '. . . sorry, about making your bed wrongly. I'm sorry we've all been so mean.'

Bianca was still fuming, but when she saw how genuinely ashamed Francesca looked, she said, 'That's OK.' It might be nice to have a true friend at last.

Maybe then she would feel like she belonged.

Chapter Six

After lunch, Bianca couldn't stand it any more. As everyone was filing back into the studio, she grabbed Cosimo's elbow and pulled him aside.

'Cosimo, I've got to go back,' she said. 'I've got to make sure Master di Lombardi is all right!'

Cosimo touched her lightly on the arm. 'I'm sure we can all visit Master di Lombardi later – but when Master Filpepi says so, and not before.'

Bianca felt desperate. 'But . . . but . . . I can work on the commissions we didn't bring with us – you *know* I'm good enough.'

Cosimo's kind expression changed. 'No, Bianca. Now stop making trouble and get back to work.'

Bianca trudged back to the stool and shrugged back into her ruffled shirt for posing, her mind racing. She wasn't going to take no for an answer. There was still work to do. She could persuade Filpepi to send her back to do it.

She just had to come up with an excuse to get out of this stupid modelling . . .

Her eye fell on Francesca's paintbrush, resting in a pot of dirty grey water.

Very casually, she bent over as if fiddling with the hem of the skirt, and then swept her arm around as she stood up, catching the edge of the dirty water pot. The pot tumbled off the counter and its contents fell in a satisfyingly disgusting splash all over one side of her skirt.

'Oh no!' Bianca gasped. 'I'm so sorry! I'll go and clean the costume, I'm so sorry!' She tore off the skirt and ran out.

As soon as she'd left the room she balled it up and threw it into a linen cupboard. She'd have to come back for it later.

Finding Filpepi was easier said than done. The enormous house, even more mansion-like in the daylight, seemed to stretch on and on in all directions. Bianca picked a likely-looking hallway and headed down it. One wall was lined with windows, and the other with works of art. They were so crammed together that the bright, creamy plaster of the wall was almost completely hidden.

Bianca paused to examine an enormous landscape painting of the view to the north from the outer city wall: rolling green and yellow fields dotted with dark scribbles of bushes and trees. A forest glowed deep green on the left hand side, and vineyards striped the hills on the right with their neat rows of grapevines.

This was a living painting, just like di Lombardi's wonderful murals – but it had Filpepi's definitive style.

48

Bianca didn't like it as much: the colours looked a little flatter, and there wasn't nearly enough detail on the closest plants. As she watched, the moving figures were already starting to repeat themselves – an eagle swooped in circles around the same treetops, and a tiny farmer with a steam-driven plough was harvesting the same part of the field over and over again.

Bianca tried hard to suppress a little thrill of pride.

My master would never have hung such a painting in his own home. He could paint a scene so realistic you'd be able to watch the seasons turn.

She walked on, past portraits of grand men and women on horseback and groups of people locked in great debates. One enchanted figure gestured wildly over a table full of scientific instruments while a group of men stood in the shadows, stroking their long beards. A little further on, a woman in a black dress held up a glowing ball of gold in one hand and a paintbrush in the other, letting the ball glint and shimmer in the light from a window. A young boy sat at her feet. The painting was called *The Artist As A Boy Learning About Light*. Bianca wondered who the woman was.

All the doors along the corridor had been firmly closed, until suddenly she turned a corner and saw that a door stood half-open between two portraits, letting a shaft of sunlight into a dim room walled with dark wood and crowded bookcases. Bianca heard the scratching sound of a pen on paper, and someone sighed. *Filpepi's study!* She stepped up to the doorway and knocked.

'Come in,' said Filpepi's voice.

Bianca pushed the door open. The room was cool and dim. It was a strangely pleasant feeling. Her eyes adjusted almost at once, and she could see that heavy curtains had been strung across the windows. The sunlight still filtered through, soft and tinged with blue.

Filpepi was sitting at a large desk, a mess of books and papers spread out in front of him and a pair of tinted eye-glasses pushed up on top of his head. Beside the desk, a ghostly white figure sat completely still, her hands folded in her lap.

Bianca blinked. Then she realized: it wasn't a real woman – it was a lifesize painting which had been propped up on the floor. She recognised it now. It was the portrait that the Grand Duchess Angelica – Duchess Catriona's great-grandmother – had commissioned for her wedding. She was wearing her wedding dress, famous for its unique beauty. It was sewn with so many diamonds it had looked like she was floating on a shimmering beam of light. At least, that was what Bianca had heard. The painting was supposed to glimmer too, in a pale imitation of the real thing. Perhaps Filpepi was restoring it for the Duchess, or more likely for the Baron da Russo. The Baron would certainly never ask di Lombardi; di Lombardi was too busy for restorations, even one as prominent as this.

Bianca wondered if that was why the room was so cool and dark. Maybe Filpepi was trying to recreate the blinding effect of the real dress.

'Can I help you?' said Filpepi, leaning forward over a

ledger covered with scribbles. 'Are you lost? It's Bianca, isn't it?'

Bianca snapped back to the real world abruptly and gave Filpepi a hasty, clumsy curtsey. 'Yes, Sir. No, Sir – I mean . . . I'm not lost. I thought, Sir, if you don't mind, I should go back to Master di Lombardi's studio. There are still commissions that need attention, Sir.'

It was an excuse, but it had the added advantage of being true. Bianca could think of at least two paintings and a sculpture she could work on. She could attend to them after she'd made sure di Lombardi was all right.

And checked for more signs of poisoning.

Filpepi regarded her for a moment and then smiled. 'That's a very good idea. I'm sure Annunzio would be very grateful for your dedication.'

'Thank you, Sir.' Bianca blushed and gave another little curtsey, and then turned to go.

'Oh, wait . . .' Filpepi called. 'Actually, there's something else you can do for me.' Bianca turned back. 'See if you can find any more of Annunzio's notebooks while you're in the house.'

Bianca frowned. 'I thought we'd brought them all with us last night, Sir.'

'Yes, that's what I thought too, but it turns out some of the notes are missing. I'd hate it if we couldn't finish Master Annunzio's commissions for want of a few sketches. Will you look for them? It may be they've slipped behind a painting or been put away for safekeeping somewhere else in the house.'

51

'I'll keep an eye out, Sir,' she said.

There was a clatter of running feet outside and the door flew open. Cosimo stood there, panting and glaring at Bianca.

'Bianca! What are you doing?' Cosimo bit his lip as he turned to Filpepi. 'I am so sorry, Sir. You must forgive her. She won't bother you any more. *Come downstairs, Bianca,*' he hissed between gritted teeth.

'It's all right,' said Filpepi with a smile. 'Bianca isn't bothering me in the slightest. In fact, she's going to return to Master Annunzio's house to run a very important errand for me.'

Bianca beamed at Filpepi. Thank goodness *someone* in this house was on her side. Filpepi dismissed them both with a wave of his hand. As soon as they were out in the corridor, Bianca stuck her tongue out at Cosimo and ran off down the corridor before he could give her a clip round the ear for being cheeky.

Chapter Seven

'Oh no, you don't!'

Bianca paused in di Lombardi's studio doorway. She looked up, cringing, to see Mistress Quinta standing on the bottom step of the stairs, blocking Bianca's path to the upper floors and di Lombardi's room.

'I see you trying to sneak up here, Bianca,' she said, folding her arms. 'I'm sure that's not why Master Filpepi sent you back, is it?'

'I just wanted . . .' Bianca began.

'He's not to be disturbed. The doctor said he must have complete rest and quiet – that means from pestering well-wishers as well. Go on. Get back to work.'

Bianca's heart sank and she made her way to the studio. Mistress Quinta stepped down, put out a work-worn hand and stopped her with a gentle squeeze on her shoulder.

'I'll have Angela bring you some tea.'

Bianca looked up at the housekeeper's exhausted,

red-rimmed eyes and gave her the brightest smile she could muster. 'Thank you,' she said gratefully.

Mistress Quinta let her go with a little pat and bustled off.

The studio was a mess. The hurry to find all of di Lombardi's sketches and notes had left drawers pulled out and cabinets flung open. Someone had knocked over a pot full of clean brushes, scattering them across the dusty wooden floor. Bianca knelt to gather them up and rinsed their bristles carefully at the wide ceramic pump sink.

The painting she'd been working on the previous day was too big to move in the cart, so it was still where she'd left it, on one of the easels by the high window. The light there was best for detail work. She reached up and pulled away the cream linen sheet that would keep the colours from being affected by air and light until they'd been fixed properly.

It was a portrait of three figures sitting together on a couch, two adults and a boy of six or seven. The Costantino family. Lord Costantino had commissioned the painting of the family to mark his tenth wedding anniversary, and suggested they be painted sitting in their favourite room – the library. Behind the three figures, bookshelves ranged up to a high ceiling, covered with hundreds and hundreds of individually painted spines of books. In fact, there were two hundred and seventeen – she'd painted most of them herself, under Cosimo's watchful eye.

The picture was almost done. She hoped Lord Costantino would be pleased. The figures needed a little more animation, and the detail on the door that could be seen in the background wasn't quite right, either. There was a panel of stained glass in the door and the light from the window wasn't glancing off it properly.

She did know how to make a *respirare* paint. She hadn't been lying to Lucia about that. But she also didn't exactly have much practice with it. Di Lombardi didn't share his secrets easily, and she probably wasn't good enough to actually use a *respirare* yet. If she tried to apply it to the figures and it went wrong, Master di Lombardi would make *her* explain to Lord Costantino why his son had swelled up like a balloon.

Bianca frowned as she turned to fetch the pots and paints and ingredients she needed. She'd stick to the window detail, and wouldn't paint the *respirare*. That way, di Lombardi would have to get better. He'd have to wake up and finish the work. He'd just have to.

She sat at a counter and poured out a selection of colours from the already mixed pots onto her favourite palette. She chose ice blue, indigo, salt chalk and sunflower. Then, being careful not to let the paint come in contact with her skin, she added a tiny drop of forest green.

Beware the green . . .

She tried to smile at the memory, but it just made her feel ill.

Putting her hand into her pocket, Bianca closed her fingers around the paintbrush that di Lombardi had handed her at the palace. She didn't quite dare to paint with it – it was his, after all. He might not even have meant to give it to her. But she enjoyed the feeling of the smooth wood, the silky hairs in the brush tickling her fingertips.

'Um,' said a voice, almost by her ear. Bianca twitched involuntarily and nearly fell off her stool. 'Angela, you scared me!' she said with a smile.

'I brought you some tea. And some bread and cheese,' said Angela.

'How is he?' Bianca asked, breaking up the crusty roll gratefully. Angela sighed and leaned on the high counter top with her chin in her hands.

'He's alive,' she said. 'He's even woken up a couple of times. But not for very long. A few seconds at most.'

'That's good!' Bianca said, through a mouthful of cheese. She swallowed hastily. 'I'm sure he'll recover.' She gave a half-laugh, determined not to let the alternative play on her mind. 'He'll have to. I don't think I can finish this without him.' She gestured lightly to the painting.

Angela stared at it. 'Do they really have that many books?' she asked, stepping a little closer. Bianca could tell from the way she turned her face that she was reading the spines, and felt proud that she'd spent so many, many hours in the library writing down the names of books so that they'd match the real collection.

'Yes. I'm adding reflections to the glass in the door,' she said. 'I'm going to make some light in a minute, and we haven't got any ready –'

Angela interrupted with a pleased gasp. 'Oh, Bianca, can I watch?' She didn't take her eyes off the painting. 'That is . . . I've always wondered . . . how do you make light and

56

movement out of nothing? I'm sure it's safe to show me, I bet I wouldn't be able to give away the secret if I tried.'

Bianca knew she wasn't supposed to talk to *anyone* about the magic except her master. Not even the other apprentices. Not even the *Duchess*. Her master had been very clear when he'd told her he was going to teach her a little of his special techniques: these secrets were for her, and her alone. She still shivered a little at the idea that he'd thought she was good enough.

But then again, perhaps they all needed to know that there was magic in the world at a time like this.

'I need to make some *shimmer*,' she said. 'Can you pass me the big red bowl from that cabinet?'

Angela skipped across the room and came back with the ceramic dish. She held her breath as Bianca lifted the lid, and then let it out in a puff of disappointment. 'Oh – it looks like ordinary sand.'

Bianca smiled. 'But see how white it is? It's very special, collected when the moon is full, and sifted so there's no bits of grit or dirt. Did you know . . . wait, I'll show you.' She got up from her stool and pulled out a contraption in which four small, round pieces of glass were held in alignment in a brass tube. Bianca twisted a key that turned a gear that adjusted the distance between the glass pieces. 'Master Lombardi invented this. He's always coming up with inventions – and this one even works!' she added, with a laugh. 'This lets us look at things really close up.' She handed the contraption to Angela, who took it as delicately as if it were made of eggshells. 'Look at the grains of sand.'

'Oh!' Angela took a step back and almost dropped the contraption. Bianca took it back gently. 'It's like looking at big glass rocks! Sand is made of glass!'

'And glass is made of sand!' Bianca glanced at Angela. She looked like her whole world had just expanded by about a hundred leagues. 'We use the way glass changes light that hits it to make the *shimmer*.'

Bianca scooped a small handful of sand out of the red bowl and dropped it onto a wide metal plate. 'You can't do this on wood or ceramic: it warps too easily.' She took a small iron tool, like a miniature shovel, from a drawer. 'Iron tools make sure the magic only goes where it's needed.' She added a tiny drop of water, mixing it with the sand.

'It . . . looks like a wet beach,' Angela said.

Bianca just smiled and picked up two pairs of goggles. Their round lenses were tinted dark blue. 'Better put these on. It won't be safe to look at it at first.' The goggles had leather straps that fitted snugly over Bianca's head. She adjusted Angela's, and then pulled on a pair of thick leather gloves.

'Just one more ingredient,' she said, going over to a metal-bound chest and lifting the lid. She took out a glass tube full of shimmering golden oil that seemed to flow and bubble around all by itself.

'What is *that*? It looks like it's alive!' Angela said, recoiling a little as Bianca carefully unscrewed the lid.

'It's called *lux aurumque*. Master di Lombardi says it

58

comes from a flower, something magical, but he won't tell me where the flower grows.' She gazed into the golden oil.

When he wakes up he can show me.

She very carefully let a single drop of *lux aurumque* fall onto the wet sand. Sparks crackled across the surface for an instant, and then the sand dissolved, melting into a single pool of liquid light.

Even with the goggles, it was incredibly bright. It pooled in the centre of the iron plate, solid and yet not solid at the same time.

'How did you do that?' Angela whispered. 'What did you do? Can anyone do it?'

'Master di Lombardi says anyone can learn,' Bianca said. She added another drop of water to the mixture. It made a high, cracking noise like breaking glass when it hit the pool of light. Angela jumped. 'But I've been learning nearly all my life, and Master di Lombardi says I'm a quick study,' she added with a proud smile. 'Master di Lombardi will not take adult apprentices, though many have asked. They aren't quite ready to believe in the same way.'

She mixed the water and light with the little shovel, and then leaned close to the plate and whispered, '*Lux aurumque, lux diffusis, lux langui.*'

Wisps of light peeled off it and vanished in the air like smoke, and the substance started to dim. She dipped the pointy end of her shovel into the indigo paint she'd been using, and touched the tiniest drop of it to the surface of the light. Colours glittered across its surface like oil on water.

Bianca peeled off her goggles and sat back. 'That's a *shimmer*,' she said.

'It's so beautiful!' Angela grinned.

She hesitated, still staring for a second, and then flung her arms around Bianca's shoulders. 'That was amazing. Thank you!' she pulled back from the hug. 'I've got to go – someone's got to get on with dinner, and Mistress Quinta could be gone for hours.'

Bianca put down her brush. 'Mistress Quinta's out?'

'Yes, she went to the market.'

'So . . . it's just you and me in the house.'

'And Master di Lombardi,' said Angela.

'Yes.' *Yes!* 'Thank you, Angela.' Bianca's heart raced. Without Mistress Quinta to stop her, she could go upstairs and see her master! She wouldn't disturb him – she just had to see for herself that he was alive.

Bianca made it to di Lombardi's floor and crossed to his door on tiptoe. She pushed it open as silently as she could and peered inside. Di Lombardi lay in the bed, his wrinkled hands folded on his chest and his silver hair brushed out across the pillow.

And there was a figure bending over him.

Chapter Eight

Bianca gawped at the stranger bending over the sickbed, shock and anger battling for control of her voice. She crept into the room, her hands out, ready to tackle him to the ground.

He was only about her age, with sticking-up brown hair, dressed in a light tunic. He looked like any one of a thousand urchins, apprentices or delivery boys she could've met on the street.

Then he raised a hand and wiped it across his cheek.

Him! It was that harlequin, the one that'd performed at the ball – the one that'd served di Lombardi the poisoned wine.

As he lowered his hand, Bianca caught the flash of steel from a short, sharp knife.

'Assassin!' she yelled, and launched herself forward.

The boy twisted to see who'd shouted just as Bianca slammed into him. She caught him off-balance, knocking him to the floor. He writhed as soon as he hit the ground, ready to roll to his feet again, but Bianca was ready for his tumbling tricks. She threw down all her weight, landing heavily on his chest. He choked, winded, as she grabbed the hand that held the knife and banged it on the floor. Finally, his grip loosened and she could pry the blade out of his fingers.

'Wait!' he gasped, as she pressed the knife under his chin.

'Who sent you? Why are you trying to kill my master?' Bianca growled.

'I'm not!' His eyes were wide and they flicked between her face and the hilt of the knife as he spoke. 'I'm not an assassin, I'm just a tumbler! My name's Marco Xavier.'

'A tumbler who just fancied breaking into a sick man's bedroom with a knife?'

The boy called Marco gulped. 'Please, just – there's an envelope. I dropped it. I was trying to find out what's wrong with him.'

It's a trick. But she'd better be sure. She knelt on the boy's legs while she glanced around – and to her surprise, there was an envelope on the floor, by the boy's right hand.

'I'm going to pick it up,' she said. 'If you try to get up I'll probably stab you by accident.'

'Fine. But be careful. Don't touch what's inside.'

Bianca hesitated, suppressing a shudder. Maybe the boy was playing with her mind. The envelope was just a little handmade square of folded paper. Bianca tried not to let her hand shake as she picked it up carefully by one corner and peered inside. There was nothing there but a smear of something white and sticky-looking.

She gave the boy a suspicious glare. 'More poison?'

'No – well, sort of. Look, I was there last night when he was poisoned –'

'You gave him the wine!' Bianca snapped.

The boy's face flushed bright red. 'I know! It's horrible! I keep thinking I should've known somehow and stopped it but it looked like any other wine, and anyway . . .' He paused for a split second, then barrelled on, 'and anyway how could I have known? But I could tell something was wrong as soon as he started choking. I don't want to be the person who killed Annunzio di Lombardi!'

Bianca's stomach twisted at the thought.

'So I came to get that.' He nodded, very carefully, towards the envelope. 'I got it off his lips. I'm sure it's arsenic!'

Bianca stared hard at the strange white substance for a few seconds.

'That makes you have fits and foam at the mouth, right? It's proof he was poisoned!'

'I'm going to let you up,' said Bianca, slipping the envelope gingerly into the pocket of her dress. Her hand brushed against di Lombardi's paintbrush again and she risked a glance at her master's face. He looked peaceful, but so pale . . .

'Come on, get up,' she said, brandishing the knife at the young tumbler. He tucked one leg under the other and rose gracefully to his feet. 'Now come with me. Slowly.'

The boy put up his hands and they edged towards the door together. She herded him, like a nervous animal, not really sure where she was taking him. But along the corridor she saw the store cupboard. And *yes*, thank the stars, the key was still hanging in the lock.

'Get in,' she said.

'But I –'

She thrust the knife forward. 'Do it!' she yelled.

He gave a yelp of dismay as she pushed him inside, slammed the door shut and locked it.

'What're you going to do now?' he demanded through the door.

'I'm coming back,' she said. 'I just have to . . . check.'

Bianca ran down the stairs and jumped half of the final flight into the studio. Her heart hammering, she grabbed a bowl and set it over a gas burner. She carefully scraped the white stuff from the envelope with the boy's knife, and added a small measure of zinc from a glass phial. The mixture bubbled and boiled, sending up steam.

Bianca's hands shook as she picked up a cold, white ceramic bowl from the mixing table and held it in the steam.

Almost at once, a nasty black stain started to creep across the clean white surface, like mould.

It was arsenic, all right.

Beware the green.

She wanted to cry.

Bianca switched off the gas and immediately took the two bowls to the sink and scrubbed them with water and alcohol until she didn't feel quite so contaminated. As she scrubbed, she thought of the boy upstairs. Who was he, really? He'd told her the truth. He'd known the signs of arsenic poisoning. But then, he'd know it was arsenic if he'd put it in her master's wine, wouldn't he?

She rinsed her hands one more time and went back up to the dorm.

'You,' she said, through the door.

'Still here,' said the boy's muffled voice.

'Where did you get the wine?' Bianca demanded.

There was no reply for a second or two. Then, just as she was taking a breath to ask again . . .

'It was the Duchess.'

Bianca gasped. 'What?'

'The Duchess Catriona gave me the bottle personally. She told me it was his favourite, and I was to make sure I gave it straight to him, and no one else.'

The words washed over Bianca, but didn't seem to mean anything. It was nonsense. The Duchess wouldn't, *couldn't*, do a thing like this. Not to her beloved art tutor.

'You're lying,' she said. 'Duchess Catriona loves Master di Lombardi.'

'You think I'd try to save my own skin by blaming the *Duchess*?' the boy asked.

'If you did you'd be pretty stupid,' Bianca mumbled to herself.

She stared at the closed door and tried to think. But everything seemed flat and unreal to her suddenly, like a painting. No – like a *bad* painting.

She breathed slowly, trying to clear her mind. If the Duchess wanted di Lombardi dead or out of the way, for some secret reason, then she could have had him thrown in prison, or killed him somewhere much less public than the first night of her Ascension festivities. So this didn't make any sense, and Bianca definitely didn't believe it.

That meant the harlequin boy was lying. But why would he tell *that* lie? And who could he be protecting? Who was scarier than Duchess Catriona when she was in a fury? Should she –

Bianca blinked.

She could smell smoke.

A second later, she heard Angela scream.

'Fire! Bianca, fire!'

Bianca stumbled down the stairs and collided with Angela. There was already smoke curling in the air around them and the floor underfoot was warm, even through Bianca's thin canvas shoes.

'There's a fire in the cellar,' Angela choked, clinging to Bianca's shoulder. 'I couldn't put it out.'

'Get outside!' Bianca pushed Angela towards the front door. 'Go! I'll bring the Master.' She made a leap back toward the stairs and di Lombardi's room. He was still sleeping, but she put her arm under his neck and tried to lift him to a sitting position. No time for a gentle awakening – she'd drag him down the stairs if she had to.

A low groan came from her master's throat, and his eyelids opened just a crack.

'Master!' Tears of joy pricked in the corners of Bianca's eyes, but she blinked them away. She threw back the covers and helped the old man swing his legs onto the floor. 'There's a fire. We've got to go, now!'

Di Lombardi gave another moan, but when she pulled him to his feet he just managed to stay upright, leaning heavily on Bianca's shoulders.

'That's it. One foot, then the other. That's it. Just one flight of stairs.' Bianca steered him to the top of the steps. The smoke had already reached the upper floor, and di Lombardi coughed weakly. Bianca paused to tear strips from the bottom of her skirt and tie one around each of their faces.

They'd made it down five steps, with the choking heat and smoke thickening all round them, when Bianca suddenly stopped.

The boy. She'd left him locked in the cupboard.

He might be a murderer, but I won't be.

'Wait here!' she helped Master di Lombardi to sit at the top of the stairs and leaned him gently against the wall, then shouted into his ear, over the growing crackling and roaring of the fire. 'I'm coming back!'

And before she could change her mind, she turned, her head down against the swirling smoke, and ran.

Chapter Nine

Her hand fumbled for the key and it nearly slipped out of her fingers, glossy with the *shimmer* that she hadn't washed off before she put it in her pocket. But she managed to get it into the keyhole and throw open the door.

'Marco!' she yelled, through her mask. The smoke rushed into the cupboard on a gust of hot air that blew Bianca's hair over her face. It filled the space completely. There was no boy inside. Bianca stared for a second, wondering if the tumbler had been some kind of magician, before the flow of smoke caught her eye. It was streaming up and out of a small slitted window. He must have climbed out when he heard Angela screaming.

Bianca knew she ought to kick herself for imprisoning an acrobat in a room with a window. Coughing violently, she turned to run back to di Lombardi.

'Wait!' The shout came from above her. 'Help me!'

She spun back. It was the boy's voice.

Bianca seized a barrel and dragged it in front of the

shelves. She clambered up on top and then shakily began to climb the last few shelves until she could lean forward and put her head through the window.

Marco was just below her, standing on the roof of a shed built onto the side of the house. It seemed as if the whole alley behind the house was alight. Flames roared out of the trapdoor to the coal cellar and black smoke billowed from all the ground floor windows.

The fire licked around the walls and the leaded roof of the shed. Marco waved frantically.

'I can't climb back up!' he gasped, jumping from foot to foot. 'My feet are already burning! I'm going to die!'

'Wait there!' Bianca yelled back.

'You keep saying that!' screamed Marco.

Bianca took a deep breath of clean air and leaned back into the smoky cupboard. There was a dustsheet folded on a shelf just on the other side of the cupboard. She could lean over and reach it. She clamped a trembling arm on to the window ledge and stretched the other out, fingers grasping. Just a little further . . .

Her foot slipped. She yelped and pulled herself back, clinging to the shelves. Her heart thundered and she made another desperate, foolhardy grab for the dustsheet. She swept it from the shelf by one corner, along with four glass bottles that tumbled to the floor and smashed, spilling oils and ingredients out onto the landing.

Bianca balled one end of the sheet up small, held the other end as tight as she could, and threw the sheet out of the window. It fluttered and unfurled in the smoke, and

69

for a second she thought it would miss, or catch on fire – a flame shot out of the kitchen window and licked around its edge. Then the boy took a leap, arms flailing, and caught it.

The sheet nearly slipped from Bianca's sweat-slick hands but she gripped on to her end with her full might. Using all her weight, she lowered herself back down the shelves and slowly onto the floor to drag the boy upwards. After a few seconds, it seemed like Marco's acrobatic training must have kicked in and the weight lessened a bit, then vanished. He toppled through the window and landed on the floor in a heap.

For a second Bianca was worried he'd hit his head but then he twisted and came up coughing. Bianca ripped off part of the sheet and thrust it into his hands, gesturing to her own mask, and he nodded and wrapped the sheet around his face. Grabbing him by the arm, she steered him through the room, out of the door and onto the landing.

Di Lombardi was still leaning where she'd left him, and still breathing, although shallowly. The smoke wasn't as bad up here as downstairs, but it was already thicker than it had been before. Bianca lifted her master onto his feet, and then felt his weight on her shoulder lessen. Through the swirling smoke and the red flashes of light from below, she could just make out the shape of Marco taking di Lombardi's other arm.

They helped him down the stairs together. The heat grew almost unbearable, so hot the sweat on Bianca's neck seemed to burn away almost as soon as it appeared. Tears streamed down her face but her eyes were stinging and bone dry.

'Shut your eyes,' she choked out. 'Keep them shut. I'll try to get us out.'

She pressed her eyes closed and felt her way as they got to the bottom of the stairs. She knew the way out to the front door – all they had to do was turn left . . .

A roaring blast of heat hit her as soon as she'd edged around the corner. A wall of flame was between them and the door. Even with her eyes closed, she could see it. She blinked her eyelids open just for a second and the shape of the flames, blocking the entrance hall, danced in front of her eyelids.

'Studio,' croaked di Lombardi. 'The . . .' he broke off and bent double, phlegm rattling in his throat.

'This way,' said Bianca.

She steered them back, over the hot floor and reached her hand out in front of her, blindly feeling for the entrance to the studio. It was, stars be thanked, a little cooler when they staggered inside, but the smoke was still thick. The windows were just vague shimmers of light in the air. Bianca put out her hand to feel her way across the room and knocked something glass to the ground with a tinkling crunch. Marco let out a yelp of pain as he walked into something and there was the wooden smack of a stool hitting the floor.

Di Lombardi was trembling all over, but he seemed to regain some of his strength – Bianca felt him put pressure on her arm, steering her towards one of the gleaming patches of light that shone through the swirling smoke.

She reached out gingerly, hoping to find her fingers meeting glass, but instead they found wood, and then warm brass – the handle of a door.

This was odd. There was no other way out of the studio. Her mind scrambled to retrace their steps through the smoke. Smashing glass and wooden stools – could they have made it to the kitchen? No – if this was the door to the coal cellar it ought to be at the heart of the fire, but the handle felt cool under her hands as she seized it and rattled and tugged at it.

'Hold still,' came di Lombardi's hoarse whisper, and then she felt him reach into her pocket. 'Hidden rooms,' di Lombardi choked out, and then spluttered something else, something Bianca couldn't catch under the creaking and cracking of the burning house and her master's laboured breath. There was a clicking noise, like the winding of a watch, and then the sound of a key fitting into a lock.

Suddenly the handle she was still holding turned. She threw open the door, helped di Lombardi across the threshold, reached out for Marco's hand to guide him inside and then stepped into the blessedly cool, smoke-free darkness and slammed the door behind her, shutting the smoke out with it.

Bianca dropped to her knees and tore the mask from her face, gasping in lungfuls of fresh, peculiar-smelling air. This wasn't the pantry or the coal cellar, after all. It was nowhere she'd ever seen before. The ground was cobbled with wide, rounded stones, just like the streets of La Luminosa – but they were in some kind of windowless indoor passageway, lit by candle sconces on the walls, and the stones were cool under her hands, not sun-warmed like the ones outdoors.

'Master?' she rubbed her eyes with the back of her hand and twisted around, looking for di Lombardi. He was on his hands and knees, his white hair hanging over his face, wild and stained grey and black with smoke. Bianca shuffled to his side and helped him to sit up straight. His face looked deathly pale and strangely unfocused, like the moon shining through thin cloud. When he spoke, only one half of his upper lip moved normally – the other twitched and went slack.

'Got to get out . . . help me . . .'

Bianca turned to snap at Marco to help her get him up, but Marco was already there, putting out a hand to take di Lombardi's right arm.

If he was an assassin, how could it be worth his while to help him? Bianca thought.

She put the thought aside for the moment and together they managed to get di Lombardi to his feet and start down the dim corridor.

As her vision cleared, Bianca started to see little bursts of colour on the stone walls, as if someone had walked down these halls carelessly swinging a paintbrush. Or a hundred paintbrushes, each with a different colour, so that it was like walking among the stars of a distant, rainbow-coloured night sky.

And it was special paint, too. There were flecks of *shimmer* and *ether*, royal purple and gold: paints no artist would have put there by accident. But it was just as strange for someone to have decorated the walls like this in a secret passage that almost nobody ever saw . . .

'What is this place?' Bianca whispered. 'I didn't know we had a secret passage in our house.'

Di Lombardi didn't answer her question.

They passed several doors, each of a different material and design, but di Lombardi shook his head and pointed them onwards. When they came to a junction where an identical corridor led away to their right and left, di Lombardi again gestured that they should go forward.

The smoke felt as if it had stained her tongue and the back of her throat, but Bianca gradually became aware of an odd smell that seemed to hang in the air all along the corridor, like that of brand new canvas after it had been stretched and treated, ready for painting.

Finally, di Lombardi spluttered, 'There,' and Bianca rushed forward to open a small door made of ancient-looking dark oak with heavy metal studs and a barred window. On the other side, she found herself stepping into a smooth, stone alcove inside a church. A tall stained-glass window cast dancing colours across the altar. Little candle flames danced on a brass rack and the familiar scent of incense and old wood filled Bianca's nostrils.

She walked a little way into the nave and looked around. She knew that pattern of light, and that collection of gleaming relics on the altar. This was the church

74

of Santa Cecilia, just around the corner from di Lombardi's studio. But why would there be a passage that linked the two?

'Master di Lombardi!' gasped Marco's voice. Bianca spun around. Her master had made it through the door, but, as she watched, he swayed and dropped to his knees on the scratchy rug in front of the altar. A key dropped out of his hand as he fell forward, clattering noisily on the stone floor.

'Master!' Bianca cried. Marco bent over di Lombardi and turned him onto his back.

'He's not breathing. Get help!' he said. He started to shake di Lombardi's shoulders and moved his head, tipping it back to check his throat was clear. Bianca turned and sprinted down the aisle, bursting through the doors at the far end into blinding sunshine and the middle of a muttering crowd.

The courtyard in front of the church was full of people, pointing and staring at a huge plume of smoke that was rising over the roofs of the buildings.

'Help!' Bianca gasped. They turned to stare at her, almost as one. 'Please help! He's not breathing!'

Father Genitivi was the first to respond, rushing inside at once, followed by another man who peeled away from the rest of the crowd like a shadow. They both swept past Bianca in a flutter of black. She ran after them, more people hurrying in on her heels.

'My god. Master di Lombardi,' said the other man, whipping off his wide black hat and kneeling at di Lombardi's side. The image was so like her memory of the doctor at the Duchess's ball that Bianca gasped, feeling dizzy. He bent over her master, peering into his eyes and pressing his fingers to his soot-blackened wrists, throat and temple, while Father Genitivi held back the rest of the curious, hopeful crowd. Some of them had turned to the great stained-glass window and were praying for Santa Cecilia to take care of di Lombardi, their hands pressed to their hearts and foreheads. Others were simply watching in shocked silence.

Bianca stood frozen, waiting for her master to splutter back to life. But something in her heart told her that he wouldn't.

The doctor sat back on his heels with a sigh.

'I'm sorry,' he said softly. 'The smoke was too much for him.' He reached out to close di Lombardi's eyes.

'No!' Bianca cried, too loud, her voice echoing in the suddenly hushed church. The crowd stared pityingly at her, or turned their faces away. Marco was the only one who looked up, right at Bianca. His face was so full of grief and anger, all of Bianca's lingering doubts melted away. She met his eyes and nodded.

This isn't a coincidence.

Someone had poisoned di Lombardi's wine last night. And when that didn't work, they set the fire to finish the job.

'Can you give us a moment, please,' she said to Father Genitivi.

He bowed low and crossed his heart, and herded the crowd away.

Bianca knelt down and took di Lombardi's wrinkled, soot-blackened hand, holding it gently.

'I don't understand any of this,' Marco whispered. 'Who set that fire? And what was that passageway we went through?'

'Is it important?' Bianca shook her head. How could he be still thinking about that when her master was murdered?

'Have you looked at where we came out?' Marco said. 'There's no door!'

Bianca looked around. She found the space where they must have come through, but there was no doorway there – it was just a line of alcoves, painted with religious scenes.

'We . . . we must have . . .' she looked around, searching for any sign of a door, but there was nothing.

She couldn't make sense of it. Her head was spinning and she couldn't focus because of all the questions in her head.

'Can you help me?' she asked Marco. 'Please. You could go back to the palace and find out as much as you can about the wine, and the Duchess.'

'Definitely,' said Marco, nodding. 'I'll do anything I can.' He got to his feet and walked out, with one last glance back over his shoulder, leaving Bianca alone in the church.

She sat for a moment. A spark of light caught her eye. Bianca knelt, hoping to find the mysterious key that di Lombardi had dropped, but it was just the paintbrush he'd given her, still shining with the faint traces of *shimmer*. It must've fallen out of her pocket.

She pressed it to her chest and held it there tightly.

I'll never, ever forget you, or everything you've taught me. I'll try to make you proud.

And I swear, I will find your killer.

Chapter Ten

Cosimo stared at Bianca as if she'd grown a second head.

'A . . . a fire?' whispered Domenico.

Bianca just stood, staring at the floor, all her words used up. She'd imagined stammering and tripping over her tongue and crying – but in the end it'd just come out. And now it was hovering in the air between them, like a ghost.

There was a fire at home. Master di Lombardi was killed.

Bianca felt pathetically glad – in the small part of her heart that could still feel glad – that Filpepi's apprentices had had the decency to shuffle out of the room when she'd walked in with soot and tears streaking her face and asked them to leave. Now Rosa and Sebastiano were both crying, but silently, as if afraid that making a sound would make it real.

Cosimo's eyes strayed to the portrait he'd been working on, watching as the child on its velvet cushion wriggled its pudgy fingers and breathed in and out in a perfect illusion of life. It was their master's final painting. Bianca could hardly bear to look at it.

'What about Angela? And Mistress Quinta?' he asked.

'They're both fine,' Bianca flushed, ashamed to have forgotten them. That good news was too much for Rosa, and she collapsed onto a stool, sobbing into her hands. Her tears seemed infectious. Bianca felt a burning at the back of her tightening throat, and Sebastiano shuffled close to Domenico, who was staring at a patch of nothing, and took his hand.

Cosimo shuddered his tears away. 'What happened?' he said, brusquely. 'Tell us everything.'

Bianca hesitated, gasping in a breath. How could she explain Marco, the arsenic and the secret passage to Cosimo and the others? She rubbed her hands over her eyes, to buy herself some time.

'I . . . I don't know how it started,' she said. 'Mistress Quinta was out, and Angela was in the kitchen. I smelled smoke and then Angela said the cellar was on fire . . .'

The door opened. Bianca's heart lightened, just a little, as Filpepi came in with another man wearing heavy soot-streaked leather breeches and a tunic. Maybe they would have some answers. And Filpepi would understand how they felt. Di Lombardi had been his master, too. Indeed, the artist's face was a sickly greenish colour and the skin over his cheeks was sunken.

'These are the apprentices,' he said to the other man, gesturing with a tired-looking sweep of his arm. 'Everybody, this is Captain Marino. Head of the Fire Watch.'

'Is the fire out, Captain?' Cosimo asked.

Captain Marino nodded slowly. His face was clean but ashes lingered in his beard. 'My men got the flames under control and put it out just before I left to come here.'

'Is there anything left?' said Domenico in a small voice.

'Not much, I'm afraid,' said the Captain. 'And I have a few questions I need to ask you.'

'Us?' Rosa gulped. 'What do you need?'

Captain Marino glanced at Filpepi, who let out a sigh and gestured for him to go on.

'A man died today. I'm sure each of you knows that this is a very serious matter. I need you all to tell me the truth.'

Bianca looked around at the other apprentices. They all exchanged miserable glances with wet eyes and drawn faces, and then nodded at the Captain.

'All right then,' the Captain nodded back sharply. 'I want you all to think about Master di Lombardi's acquaintances, his friends and enemies, anyone he worked with, or for. Anyone who recently commissioned a painting or modelled for him. Anyone at all, who might have seemed to act . . . suspiciously.'

Bianca bit back a gasp.

He knows it wasn't an accident. Of course he does!

'Suspiciously?' Sebastiano frowned at Rosa. She shrugged back.

'I'm sorry, Captain, I don't know quite what you mean.'

The Captain sighed. 'Then forgive me, but I must be blunt. Do any of you know anyone who would want to hurt Master di Lombardi? Who might want to destroy his work? Who might even want to kill him?'

The other apprentices looked at each other, pale with shock.

'The fire in the cellar seems to have been set deliberately,' the Captain went on, while Bianca's mind raced. Here, finally, she had the chance to tell someone what had been pressing on her heart for the last day. She could tell him about the poisoned wine and he might believe her.

But . . .

Her heart sank again. It was all very well setting the authorities on the trail of the murderer, but how could she tell him what she suspected – that Duchess Catriona herself had been involved in all this?

The other apprentices were each shaking their heads now.

'Sorry, no,' murmured Sebastiano.

'Who would do such a thing?' Rosa sniffed.

'I understand,' said the Captain, scratching his beard. 'Tell me . . . was di Lombardi a hard master? Did he ever mistreat you at all?' Seeing the frowns of the apprentices, he went on. 'You know, there is no shame in speaking ill of the dead if the dead haven't been kind to us in life.' If the Captain meant his smile to be warm, he had failed. 'We know that di Lombardi wasn't an easy man to get along with. Perhaps he beat you, or held back your wages. Masters do, all the time, I believe. If any of you resented him, nobody would think any the less of you.'

There was a shocked silence. Captain Marino had spoken

airily, simply, as if it didn't matter one bit how the apprentices felt. But he was betrayed by his eyes. Bianca spotted the gleam of suspicion in their depths and balled her fists in her dress pockets to stop him seeing them tremble.

Cosimo's jaw had gone slack, but his eyebrows drew in angrily, and he pulled himself up to his full height, though he barely reached the Captain's shoulder.

'Master di Lombardi was . . . was a fair, kind man; a great artist and a great teacher . . .' his voice tightened. 'And you're asking if one of *us* set the fire that killed him?'

Captain Marino's eyes narrowed. 'Now then, there's no need to get defensive, is there? Is there perhaps something you'd like to tell me? What's your name, son?'

'This is absurd!' burst out Filpepi. He ran his hands through his hair, plastering it back to his scalp. 'They're barely more than children! And in any case, every one of them was here, under my supervision, all morning – except for Bianca.'

The Captain's piercing gaze flew from Cosimo's face to Bianca's. Bianca fought the urge to take a step backwards.

'And what were *you* doing at the house?' Captain Marino asked.

Bianca hesitated, torn, imagining pouring the whole truth out to the Captain, and then imagining him taking it all wrong. 'I . . . I . . .'

'How dare you? She tried to save poor Annunzio's life!' Filpepi stepped between the apprentices and the Captain and threw out a pointing finger towards the door. 'I won't have it. Get out of my house, and don't come back until you've learned some manners.'

Captain Marino's eyes fell on Bianca. Her hand closed on di Lombardi's paintbrush in her pocket and she held it tight, her heart beating unevenly. There was no use trying to convince him of her story now. He'd assume she was covering for herself and have her thrown in jail.

Captain Marino saluted Filpepi casually and walked out of the studio.

'I'm so sorry,' Filpepi told the apprentices. 'I should never have let him in.'

'Sir,' said Cosimo. 'Our housekeeper, Mistress Quinta, and the kitchen girl, Angela, do you know what will happen to them?'

Filpepi smiled. 'I'll see that they're taken care of,' he said. 'If I can't find a job for them in my household I'll make sure they find other employment. Don't worry.'

'Thank you, Sir,' Cosimo said with a bow.

Bianca picked up a stick of charcoal and began to sketch as Filpepi's apprentices came back into the room. Gabriella glanced at Filpepi to see his back was turned then pretended to stumble as she walked past Bianca, knocking the charcoal from her hand. Lucia sniggered quietly.

Annoyance burned the back of Bianca's throat – why did she ever think they'd behave decently? But Bianca simply fetched a second stick of charcoal from the drawer.

It was much worse for Domenico. He was using a scrap of spare canvas to practise his painting, and the moment he looked away, Bianca saw Gennaro lean against it.

'Careful!' shouted Domenico.

'I'm so sorry, Domenico,' Gennaro sneered. 'Were you using that?'

'What's going on over there?' Filpepi called from the other side of the room.

Domenico's carefully painted landscape blurred into a horrid brown mess. His face crumpled. Bianca could see he was fighting not to cry. 'Nothing, Sir.'

'Are you all getting on well?' Filpepi asked, his brow furrowed.

'Very well, Master,' said Lucia smartly.

Bianca could see Cosimo's annoyance and his urge to tell on her in the twitch at the corner of his eye, but he kept quiet.

'Good.' Filpepi gave her a curt nod and stepped up to inspect the painting Gennaro was working on, a seascape of the harbour with several tall ships. Bianca thought it was pretty good, actually. The sea was moving quite convincingly and the light was nice. But Filpepi looked at the painting, glared at Gennaro and seized a paintbrush. He dipped it in white paint and, to Bianca's shock, set about crossing out parts of the picture. 'No. No. This is terrible. This sky is fine, but you'll need to start again with this ship. Have you ever *seen* a ship, Gennaro?'

Gennaro looked miserable, but stared straight ahead and didn't answer.

'Just not good enough,' Filpepi said, shaking his head and moving on to the next painting.

Bianca flushed. Was her judgement of Filpepi so far off?

Filpepi moved between his apprentices, criticising their work. Their paintings weren't perfect, but Filpepi's criticisms were harsh, and his praises were few and far between.

'Lucia, your horse looks like a fat cow. Master Danieli asked for *majestic*. And Ezio, I see no life in this painting, no spark. Re-do it, please.' He tipped cleaning fluid over Gabriella's painting so it dripped. 'Gabriella, what have I told you about light and space?'

Bianca was getting more and more uncomfortable. This wasn't how Master di Lombardi had run his studio at all. He'd been stern and strict, but never *harsh*. He never pointed out a flaw without at least giving them some idea of how to fix it . . .

'Francesca, let's see what you've managed to do to this today.' Filpepi sounded defeated before he even looked at the painting Francesca had been working on.

Bianca frowned, holding her breath. Would he notice any trace of the mistake from this morning?

'Hmm.' Filpepi leaned in close to the painting for a second. 'This is actually not too bad, Francesca. In fact, I'd say this is the best you've ever painted. Well done.'

Bianca smiled to herself and looked away, proud of the fact that she'd earned a compliment from Filpepi. She didn't mind that Francesca was taking the credit.

'Yes, Master, Francesca has much improved under my tutelage,' said Lucia, stepping forward. Bianca sighed. She caught Francesca's eyes. Bianca held up a hand and gave a tiny shake of her head.

It doesn't matter, she mouthed.

86

Francesca frowned, and then raised her chin defiantly. 'Actually, Master . . .' Lucia glared at Francesca for daring to speak but Francesca continued. 'Bianca's the one who did this.'

Filpepi stared at her, and Francesca wilted slightly, but went on. 'I'm – I'm trying to get better. Bianca's the one who helped me.'

Lucia turned her glare on Bianca; it felt like the heat of the sun. But Filpepi gave Bianca a much cooler look.

'Oh really?' he said thoughtfully. 'Well, the painting is good. Let's hope some of Bianca's lessons stick.' He hesitated, staring at Bianca for a second, and then looked away. 'You're all dismissed for the day. Cosimo, why don't you take the others to the chapel for mass?'

Cosimo gave a smart nod and ushered di Lombardi's apprentices out of the room. Bianca glanced back and saw that Filpepi was looking at her again. She felt his gaze as she walked from the room. Bianca couldn't tell if he was pleased or upset with her.

Chapter Eleven

Bianca allowed herself to be swept along with the others as they pulled on their cloaks and headed out of Filpepi's house. But as soon as they'd passed out from under the fragrant, mottled shadows of the orchard she hung back. Cosimo led the group right, towards the spire of San Orlando's, and she waited until they'd turned the corner and then strode away, head down, across the bridge, back towards di Lombardi's house – at least, the site that had been his house.

The damage was worse than she'd been expecting. The stone front of the building was mostly intact, but so blackened with smoke and soot that it was like a huge wet lump of coal. Water streamed down from the upper floors, dripping a lake of dirty black water onto the street. The windows had cracked or melted out of their charred frames, and the front door was gone, leaving a dark wet space, like a cave mouth in a fairy tale.

Bianca ducked inside, feeling her way carefully along

the creaking floorboards of the hall, afraid they might have burned through. But it looked like someone had already been here. Wet ash was piled up against the walls, as if it'd been swept. Bianca placed her feet a bit more certainly, deciding that if the floorboards had held up Captain Marino and the Fire Watch stomping in their heavy wet leather tunics and helmets looking for the source of the blaze, they must be able to support her weight.

The smell wasn't too bad until she stepped into the studio. There her throat closed up and she bent double, coughing into her hands. Her vision dimmed, swirling greyness crept up over her, and she could feel panic battering at her.

It's all over. There's no smoke. It's over.

Bianca forced herself to straighten up and open her watering eyes. The smell was still terrible. Paint had peeled and flaked and burned, leaving behind chemical and alchemical scents that seemed to crawl inside her nose and take up residence. She held her sleeve over her mouth as she stepped inside.

The painting of Lord Costantino and his family had almost completely burned away. All that work, all those hours spent carefully lettering the spines of two hundred and seventeen books – gone in a few minutes. Most of the cabinets were destroyed, instruments and ingredients scattered across the floor. Twisted iron tools with no handles surrounded the wooden statue of a tree that di Lombardi had been working on. Amazingly, it had survived almost intact. Its cracked, blackened surface looked . . . almost beautiful.

Glass crunched underfoot, and Bianca flinched as she stepped over a fallen stool. She hesitated. Falling glass, and a toppled stool – did that mean the mysterious door *was* in the studio somewhere? She spun around, searching, and then circled the room, tapping on the walls and listening for a hollow sound. But there was no sign of any door.

'Is there anything we can save?'

Bianca spun around. Master Filpepi stood in the doorway, a black handkerchief held over his nose. Bianca flushed and gave him a hasty curtsey, fixing her eyes on the ashy floor.

'I'm sorry, Sir. You must forgive –'

'I don't blame you for coming back here,' Filpepi said. 'It's all right, Bianca, you can look up.'

Bianca slowly raised her eyes to meet his. 'I – I wanted to try to find out what happened,' she said.

'I couldn't believe it, either.' Filpepi took another step into the room and looked around at the destruction. His gaze seemed distant, somehow, as if the sadness of it was too much for him to feel properly. 'I've known Master Annunzio all my life. He was such a tough old bird. A real survivor. And then breathing in smoke, of all the things to finally . . .' he broke off and his face twitched into a rueful smile. 'I'm sorry, I'm rambling, please, ignore me.'

'Oh no, I don't mind,' Bianca blurted out. She blushed. 'That is – I feel the same.'

'Bianca, I've been thinking,' said Filpepi. 'I see a lot of myself in you.'

'Really?' Bianca blinked, her heart in her throat.

'Oh yes. You're the youngest apprentice – the last of di Lombardi's – that can't be easy, sometimes. I expect the others are hard on you.'

Bianca looked away, feeling herself blush, but her heart lifted a little. It was as though Filpepi had a window into her life!

'Yet you're obviously talented. I think perhaps you should come to me for some tuition.'

'Oh!' Bianca couldn't believe what she was hearing. 'That . . . that would be . . . wonderful!' Bianca gasped.

'Good.' Filpepi turned another smile on her. 'So, did you find anything we can save?'

'I – I think Count Benedetti would like to have this,' she said, indicating the charred, twisted wooden tree. Filpepi picked up the fluttering remnant of a linen cover and lifted the statue, cradling it in his arms.

'I'll make sure he gets it. But nothing else? No paintings, sketches, notebooks? Anything?'

Bianca let out a heavy breath and looked around. 'I don't think anything else survived. It's all just . . . ash.' She swallowed back the lump in her throat.

Filpepi gave her a strained, kind smile. 'I want to have a look at the damage for myself. It pains me to be so cynical, but clerks will come soon to assess the house, and I'd hate them to cheat whoever inherits this place by saying it's in a worse state than it is. I'll be upstairs if you need me.' He turned, and then looked back. 'Don't spend too long here. It doesn't do to dwell. Just collect what you can save and come away, eh?' He picked his way out, carefully manoeuvring the tree statue through the dripping doorway.

When he'd gone, Bianca walked one more time around the edges of the room. She trained her eyes on the wreckage, trying to suppress the urge to search for equipment she could salvage. There was some – the odd unbroken ceramic bowl, a few brushes that'd been safely shut in a drawer – but that wasn't what she was looking for.

'There must be some clue,' she muttered under her breath. 'Something out of place. Somewhere to *start*.'

She trailed her fingers over the wall as she walked. They bumped over the grooves between the huge stones. *Bump bump bump . . . bump.*

Bianca hesitated, and looked back.

Her eyes told her that there was a dip between the two stones, a small gap filled with grainy mortar. But her fingers had passed over it smoothly.

She ran a hand over the area, and there it was again – her hand felt nothing, though her eyes were still saying there was a gap.

It's an illusion! There's something here.

She put both hands up on the wall and felt around. At last her fingers found an invisible edge and she pressed against it. Something went *click*. There was a brief sound of clacking, like gears turning, and then part of the wall swung out on a well-oiled hinge.

Bianca gasped. This wasn't her mysterious door – it was just a square hole, cut into the wall. How many secret hiding places did her master have around the house? She put her hand into the darkness and found something that rustled.

It was a pile of small notebooks, bound in black and brown leather and tied up with string. She took them out and shut the door. The secret door slotted back into place without a sound, as if there had never been anything there.

These must be the notebooks Filpepi was looking for, Bianca thought. She took in a breath to call for him, and then hesitated.

These were some of the very last things she had that belonged to her master. His hands had written and drawn in these pages. These were his private papers. But surely he wouldn't mind her looking at them? *What does it matter now he's dead?* she thought sadly. Pulling up a still fairly intact stool to one of the counters, she sat down and undid the string on the first notebook.

She frowned down at the designs on the first few pages for a moment, and then a laugh bubbled up and escaped her lips. There wasn't a single page devoted to di Lombardi's work – not his paid work, anyway. There were no cartoons for paintings, or sketches for statues. There weren't even any of di Lombardi's accounts.

These were his inventions. The ones that almost never worked. Most of these, Bianca didn't think he'd even built prototypes for. They were mad, every one of them.

She found sketches for *Vehicle for Traversing Underneath the Canal Surface*, a tiny one-person steamcart that could navigate under the water. The next page showed a detailed diagram of a large disc made from leather and wire that was labelled as a *Machine to Amplify the Sound of a Violin*. Further on there was a series of pages devoted to creating artificial arms and legs, even delicately carved and painted wooden hands that could reach and grasp objects just by forming a magical bond with the thoughts of the wearer.

A fond smile creased the corners of Bianca's mouth as she flipped through the book. She ran her fingers over the sketches on a page titled *Necessary Parts for a Flying Machine* – wheels, gears, steam pumps, inflatable bladders, a huge pear of leather wings, and twisty glass-and-copper things that she couldn't even name.

These weren't the notebooks Filpepi wanted, these were the result of di Lombardi's creativity running mad. It wouldn't do any harm for her to keep them.

Bianca closed the book and held it close to her chest for a minute, like a child with a favourite doll. Master di Lombardi might have been strict, he might have seemed reclusive and grumpy to the outside world, but this, here, was the man she knew. The artist, the genius, the kind man who never stopped working and dreaming and making things. She would keep the notebook, to remind her how he would have been pleased that she wasn't neglecting her own work. Filpepi was going to give her special tuition.

At least, now something was going right.

Chapter Twelve

The next morning Bianca knocked on the door of Filpepi's study.

'Come in,' he called, and Bianca opened the door and went inside. It was still cool and dark, curtains drawn across the windows against the morning sunshine, and the painting of the Grand Duchess's gown was still sitting on its easel beside his desk.

'Good morning, Bianca. I have something very special for you to work on,' said Filpepi, gesturing to her to take a seat on the other side of the desk.

Bianca's heart soared – it couldn't be the painting of the gown, could it? But she forced herself to be calm. She was sure he just meant a special exercise he'd come up with. He wouldn't let her work on something so important!

'Did you enjoy the second night of celebrations last night, Sir?' Bianca asked politely.

Filpepi shook his head. 'You didn't hear? The Duchess

95

cancelled the ball as a mark of respect. This evening's performance should go ahead as planned, but she said she couldn't bear to celebrate after poor Annunzio's death.'

Bianca's heart twisted. That sounded like the Duchess Catriona she knew – not someone who would ever poison and suffocate her beloved master.

'Do you know this painting, Bianca?' Filpepi said, gesturing to the Grand Duchess Angelica.

'Oh yes!' Bianca gasped. 'Isn't it wonderful? It's Master Quirelli's great masterpiece!' Bianca knew the story: Quirelli gave up his position as Royal-Artist-In-Residence after he finished it, saying he would never better the piece. 'But . . . you don't want *me* to help you work on it, do you?'

'Of course I do,' said Filpepi. 'It'll be good for you to learn from the old masters.' He drew his chair to the side of the easel and looked up at the Grand Duchess. 'I'm working on restoring it, but I want it to be even better than before – I want the dress to look and feel real.' Bianca could see how passionate he was as he spoke. 'Now . . . how would you handle adding real sparkle to the dress?'

Bianca's heart hammered in her chest. 'I . . . er . . . I'm not sure I'm the best person –'

'Don't panic,' said Filpepi kindly. 'It isn't a test. Just be confident. What would Master Annunzio do?'

Bianca took a few deep breaths and then approached the painting, examining the brilliant white of the satin and the dots of rainbow-coloured reflections that sparkled off each of the thousands of diamonds.

'Well . . . it'd have to be a very strong *glimmer*, at least twice as much *lux aurumque* as I'd normally use,' she said slowly. 'For the cloth, I'd make extra sure the paint felt smooth, but not hard. I'd add to the general shape of the dress around the edges . . .' she put out a hand to point and then drew it back again quickly.

'It's all right,' said Filpepi. 'Show me.'

'Here,' she pointed with a trembling hand to the bottom of the dress. 'If I wanted to make it feel really solid, I'd add two parts *ether* to one part satin white and make sure that every fold is exactly the right shade. And for the diamonds – it's just a guess – but I might add . . . *real* crushed diamonds.' Bianca instantly felt stupid. As if they would use real diamonds! 'Although . . . no. The expense wouldn't –'

'Very good,' said Filpepi, with a smile. 'Exactly correct.'

Bianca swelled with pride. 'Really?'

'Oh yes. In fact, why don't you see if you can make a *glimmer* strong enough for me now? If I think it's good enough I may even let you begin to work on the painting.'

Bianca thought she was going to faint as he walked over to a sideboard and opened it to reveal a small workbench stocked with everything she would need. There was even a drawer of powdered diamond! This was better than she could possibly have hoped for. She was going to learn so much from Master Filpepi. Maybe life with him wouldn't be so bad.

*   *   *

Bianca felt awkward taking her seat at the luncheon table with the others. They'd been working away all morning while she was with Filpepi.

'No wonder he has to give her extra lessons,' said Gabriella, in a whisper that carried all the way down to where she sat. 'He must be trying to figure out if she's good for anything at all. I don't know why he bothers, though – surely she'll be the first one to go.'

Why are you so mean? Bianca wondered, glaring at Gabriella, but she didn't rise to the other girl's bait. Her morning of working with Filpepi had been wonderful. She'd mixed several batches of magical paints and had even been allowed to paint the lace cuffs on the Grand Duchess's sleeves – fiddly, difficult work.

'What do you mean, the first one to go?' Rosa demanded.

Gabriella turned a smug smile on her. 'Well, Master Filpepi obviously has to let *someone* go. He's got twice as many apprentices as he needs now.' She said this as if it were nothing. 'I expect you'll all be out on the street within a week. And little Miss *I can paint a respirare* over here is the youngest, so she'll be the first out the door.'

Despite herself, Bianca felt a jolt of anxiety in the pit of her stomach. Could it be true? If it was decided by age, she'd be out. But then she shook herself. She couldn't let Gabriella bully her like this! She knew she was good. And besides . . .

'I've been an apprentice my whole life,' she said, only adding *sort of* in her head. 'Master di Lombardi –'

'Oh shut up about your precious master. He was a stuffy

old goat who didn't even teach you properly,' Gabriella snapped.

'Our master was twenty times the artist or teacher Filpepi will ever be! I know it. You know it. And the whole of La Luminosa –'

'Bianca!' Sebastiano hissed, his eyes fixed on the kitchen doorway behind Bianca's head.

She turned, dreading what she would see. It was Filpepi himself, glaring at them all with a face like stone. He had heard what she said. Bianca's face burned.

'I will not stand for arguing among my apprentices,' he growled. '*Every one* of you is here only until I decide you should go. You would do best to remember that. Bianca, come here.'

Bianca forced herself to stand and turn and walk towards him, though her legs felt like they were carved from marble.

'I have a job for you,' he said. 'I want you to take care of one of your master's unfinished murals in the palace.' He held out a sheaf of sketches. Bianca took them, almost in a daze. Was this really happening to her? There was an impressed murmur from di Lombardi's apprentices, and a shocked one from Filpepi's.

'Follow me,' Filpepi said, and Bianca half-ran after him out of the room.

'Master Filpepi, Sir, please,' she said when they were out in the hallway. Filpepi turned and fixed her with a cool stare. 'Um – I'm really sorry,' she said. 'I didn't mean what I said.'

Filpepi sighed. 'Yes, Bianca, I think you did. But I don't think you should apologise to me. After all . . . you were right. I'm nowhere near Master di Lombardi's standard. Not yet.' He reached out and gave her a friendly pat on the shoulder. 'We are all learning. Always.' And with that he walked away, leaving her standing, rather stunned, clutching a pile of sketches.

Bianca didn't know what she had done to get so lucky. Not only was she forgiven by her new master, she'd been honoured by him as well. And the best part was that she'd be back at the palace, which meant the hunt for di Lombardi's murderer was far from over!

Bianca stood in the Rose Gallery, her large leather case of tools and paints open beside her. Leaning close to the mural, she examined the work that had already been done. The Gallery was one of the corridors along one side of the palace. One wall was lined with large windows that let in the sunshine. The painting took up almost the whole length of the other wall.

It was a picture of a beautiful hothouse, with rows of earth beds raised from an ochre-tiled floor. A rainbow of different coloured rose bushes grew in the beds. When it was finished, warmth and light and the scent of roses in bloom would flood the Gallery. There would be about an arm's length of real, magical space that anyone could reach into and run their fingers over the soft, silky petals.

Bianca stepped back and let out a small sigh. She was where she needed to be, inside the palace, but she really needed to sneak around to look for clues. Doing that and finishing this mural seemed an impossible task.

A lot of the work had been done, but there was still so much to do, and most of it way beyond the level of difficulty she normally handled. She took di Lombardi's paintbrush – her paintbrush, now – from her pocket and twirled it between her fingers as she tried to decide where to begin. She picked a part of the painting inside the space that people could reach into. Some space had been added already, so it wasn't quite like painting on a flat surface. She had to focus hard on trusting what her eyes told her, not how her hands felt as they reached in to paint the door to the hothouse. She wasn't sure how much time had passed, but the door was beginning to look and feel solid under her brush when she heard light footsteps coming into the Rose Gallery.

'Oh – Marco!' Her heart skipped a beat, half-excited to see him, half-apprehensive. Had he found anything out about Master di Lombardi's death?

The tumbler gave her a small wave, like a half-salute, and smiled – though he didn't look particularly happy.

'Back to work already,' he said.

Bianca flushed. 'It's what my master would've wanted . . .'

'Oh, I didn't mean that. It's good. It's good to have something to do.'

Bianca carefully washed her brush in a diluted solution of paint-remover and dried it on her apron. 'Any news . . .?'

Marco walked down the Gallery and hopped up to perch on one of the windowsills, kicking his feet against the wall. Bianca suppressed a flinch – it might only be a pink wash with simple rose-pattern edging, but someone had painted that wall.

'No proof of anything, no,' said Marco.

'Clues?' Bianca twisted the brush between her fingers. '*Anything?*'

'Well . . . not really.'

Bianca walked over to lean on the wall beside him. 'What does that mean?'

'It's the Duchess,' said Marco. Bianca's heart gave a judder but she tried to keep her face impassive. 'She seems so . . . different. Ever since the first night of the celebrations, she's been cold. Distant. As if she just doesn't care about anything any more.' Bianca frowned. That was rather odd . . . 'She's taking absolutely *no* interest in the troupe!' Marco finished wistfully.

Ah. Bianca suddenly understood Marco's comment about work. The restless way his fingers were drumming on his knees showed he was bored; the Duchess no longer wanted the troupe to perform for her. Still, Bianca wasn't sure this was much of a clue. Just because the Duchess had lost interest in one of her entertainments, didn't mean it was connected to her master's murder.

'Maybe she's just sad about Master di Lombardi?' she suggested.

Marco gave a hard shake of his head, making his tight black curls bounce around his ears. 'No. Not like this. You knew the Duchess before – would you expect her to grieve quietly?'

Bianca tried to imagine the Duchess's reaction to a favourite courtier's death, and had to admit she was imagining more flaring temper, weeping and black drapes everywhere than dignified silence. 'Maybe not.'

'But she's so quiet. She's just sitting on the throne or in her chambers not talking to anyone. You know the festivities are back on this evening? I was with Father when he went to tell her about the play we've planned for it and invite her to the rehearsal, and . . .'

'And?' Bianca prompted, breathlessly.

'She just *looked* at him, and said, "I do not wish to attend your rehearsal," and then gazed out of the window. I don't understand! She once had a stand-up fight with the Baron da Russo because he thought it wasn't seemly for her to watch us practise! We were right there watching them argue. Father tried to hurry us out, but she wouldn't let us go. She said she didn't give two hoots for what he thought was seemly; she wanted to watch. How could she just suddenly not care any more?'

Bianca shook her head. She could hardly imagine the Duchess being so cool. But she couldn't imagine her ordering her master to be killed, either. 'Do you think . . . it could be a guilty conscience?' she asked slowly.

'Honestly, I don't know,' Marco shrugged.

Bianca bit back a sarcastic comment about how helpful that was. 'Well, we've got to work it out. We have to come up with a . . . a test, to see what she's thinking about.'

'But what can we do? I'm not sure about simply asking

103

her, "Your Highness, have you ordered any poisonings recently?"'

Something in Bianca's brain fizzed. She looked up at Marco, who recoiled.

'I'm *not* asking her that!' he said.

'Yes, you will – except not so simply. You said you're performing for her this evening. You can make some kind of reference to a poisoning in the play! Can't you?' Marco gave Bianca a very sceptical look, but she ploughed on. 'You can do a routine about someone getting poisoned and collapsing, and then you'll see what she looks like when she sees it. If she looks guilty, or gets really angry, we'll know it hit a nerve.'

'I don't know. I'd have to persuade the rest of the troupe. I'm not sure they'll go for it.'

'Aren't plays always full of poisonings and murders?' Bianca asked.

'Well, yes, that's true,' Marco said thoughtfully. 'Actually, my father has written a play with a poisoning in it, but –'

'Come on, then!' Bianca grabbed Marco's sleeve – then dropped it and turned back to make sure she hadn't left the lids off the pots of paint – then grabbed it again. 'Where are they now? Let's go!'

The players were rehearsing in one of the ballrooms. Bianca still felt a bit awed as she watched two women performing cartwheels along the room in perfect unison and a young man dangling upside down from a long rope by only his ankle. Master Xavier was watching and giving notes, at the same time as talking to a young woman dressed like a princess in a blue velvet gown. She had a mass of golden curls under a wooden crown that'd been painted silver.

'Father!' Marco said, running up to them. Master Xavier looked down.

'Marco, there you are. You're late. Get changed at once, we need you to rehearse the big ballroom scene . . .' his eyes fell on Bianca. 'And who is this?'

'My name is Bianca, Sir,' Bianca said, curtseying. 'I'm a friend of Marco's,' she added. 'I – well, *we* – we wanted to ask you something. As a favour.' Bianca straightened up as inspiration struck her. 'A favour to Duchess Catriona!'

'Oh?' Master Xavier turned and leaned on his striped staff. 'What kind of a favour?'

Anything for the Duchess; Bianca had his full attention. 'Is it right that you wrote a play, about a poisoning, called, um . . .' she shot Marco a desperate glance.

'She means The Poisoning of the Tortured King, father,' he said.

'I did,' said Master Xavier. 'But – the Duchess hasn't heard of my writing, surely?'

'Oh but she has!' said Bianca, nodding emphatically. 'She told me it was the best play she's read in the last year. Maybe ever! And she said she would just *love* it if you would perform it for her at the Ascension festivities tonight.'

Master Xavier stroked his short pointy beard. 'Of course! I'd love to, we all still know our parts. But I don't know if we've got the right props here . . .'

'Actually, I think we might,' said the young woman, taking off her crown and the golden curls, revealing cropped black hair underneath, which she scratched thoughtfully. 'We can use the set from The Poor Prisoner and most of the costumes are the same as in Twice The Fool.' She gestured to herself. 'I'm even dressed for the Princess already!'

'Then I can tell the Duchess you'll do it?' Bianca asked breathlessly.

Xavier smiled. 'Absolutely! It would be my pleasure,' he said, sweeping her a low bow.

Bianca curtseyed again, and gave Marco a sneaky thumbs-up.

'I have to get back to work. Meet me in the Rose Gallery after the performance,' she whispered. Marco returned the thumbs up.

Bianca ran back to the Rose Gallery, feeling light on her feet and rather lightheaded too. She couldn't quite believe what they'd just done – but if it revealed anything about the Duchess, anything at all, it would be worth it.

She wiped down the paintbrush and moved to dip it into the mixture of green and *saltatio* that she'd prepared earlier, to keep working on the outlines of leaves outside the greenhouse . . .

But the paint was gone. The whole pot of *saltatio* was just not there any more. Bianca spun around, searching the windowsills, the floor, the space under the stool – she even leaned her head into the greenhouse mural to check behind the rose bushes. But it was no good. The *saltatio* was missing.

106

Bianca let out a long moan. 'What'll I do?' she groaned. 'Oh god, it's so expensive . . .' Lucia had made it very clear when she'd left that any of the magic paint that she took out of Filpepi's house *must* be returned, even if it was empty. She'd said the paint wasn't to be left alone, even for a moment.

And Bianca had just run off and left it lying around where anyone could take it.

Despite the light and space from the painting in front of her, Bianca felt like the walls were closing in. What could she do? If she admitted she'd left the painting, they'd ask her why. And what if she had been seen going to talk to the players? What if their performance was traced back to her lie about the Duchess?

There's only one thing to do. She had to get some more *saltatio.* Which meant . . . she had to make some – something she had never done before. She'd only seen Master di Lombardi make it once, months ago. Bianca swallowed.

She had to try.

Chapter Thirteen

There was a small painting studio inside the palace, kept for the official Royal-Artist-In-Residence. It was only a few corridors from the Rose Gallery, and Master di Lombardi had always kept some extra supplies there so that he didn't have to send someone to his own studio if he needed anything.

As she raced along the corridors Bianca prayed that he'd left some *lux aurumque* there. Otherwise, there would be no magic, and no *saltatio*, and she might as well have her own head cut off right now . . .

The studio was barely bigger than a cupboard – an impression that was even more accurate considering that all four walls were completely lined with shelves. Bianca barged in and dragged a chair up against the door to keep it shut.

'*Lux, lux*, come on, *lux aurumque* . . .' she muttered, and then let out a yelp of joy. There on the top shelf she could see a slight movement of light. She climbed up on another chair and fished the small glass pot down. There was barely enough of the magic golden oil to make one small batch of *saltatio*. She'd have to get it right first time.

All right, she said to herself. *You can do this. Possibly.*

She shook herself, grabbed a pot of powdered bone and a large metal bowl and spoon, and started to mix. She needed to keep the mixture continuously moving while she added a pinch of yeast and a splash of water. The cupboard size of the studio actually came in handy when she realized she'd left the second-to-last ingredient on the shelf. She held the spoon at arm's length and stretched out, just seizing the jar full of moonflower pollen between her fingertips. She tipped a small shake of the pollen into the mixture, and then carefully, stirring all the while, uncorked the glass of *lux aurumque* and poured its whole contents into the bowl.

The mixture swirled, bubbled, roiled like a restless sea. Bianca took a deep breath, removed the metal spoon, and blew a long, steady stream of air over the surface.

'*Saltatio, magica, saltatio!*' she whispered.

The white mixture stopped moving.

Now to find out if I've made something magical – or just wasted several priceless ingredients.

She took out a piece of spare paper from a drawer, dipped her paintbrush into the paint and very carefully drew a little stick figure in the middle of a jump.

Nothing happened . . . until she raised her brush from the paper. Bianca yelped and reared back as the stick figure abruptly came to life. It jumped up and down on the page, like an athlete trying to set a record.

'I did it,' Bianca breathed. She watched the little figure jumping for a few more seconds, and then leapt into a jump herself, punching the air. 'I did it!'

I made movement, all by myself. I made life!

Bianca grinned, folded the jumping stick man up and slipped him carefully inside her pocket, then hurriedly scraped the *saltatio* into a pot. She wouldn't get in trouble now. But more importantly, she had mastered the magical technique. There was no way, absolutely no way, that she would get thrown out on the street when she showed Filpepi what she could do!

She ran from the tiny studio and sprinted back to the Rose Gallery. Everything was going to be fine. She even allowed herself to skip a little as she turned the final corner . . .

Smack!

Bianca gasped and fell backwards, landing awkwardly on her hands. She looked up to see what she'd run into, and chills ran through her whole body.

Duchess Catriona was standing over her, with white *saltatio* paint splashed across the front of her red velvet gown. Two guards loomed behind her, and beside her stood the Baron da Russo, glaring down at Bianca, his face going red.

'Your Highness Duchess Catriona! Baron da Russo! I'm so sorry.'

Bianca scrambled to her feet, clamping her hand across the top of the *saltatio* pot.

'So you should be!' shouted da Russo. 'This is a palace, not a child's playground.'

Bianca gave Duchess Catriona a small, weak smile, praying that the Duchess was in a good mood, that she'd remember how much she liked di Lombardi's apprentices, and that Bianca wasn't about to be on the sharp end of one of her screams of rage.

But the Duchess didn't seem to have noticed the state of her dress. She barely even stopped walking.

'Duchess?' Bianca asked weakly.

As soon as Bianca had got up out of her way the Duchess swept gracefully by like a canal boat under sails, her back straight and her eyes set on the door at the other end of the Gallery. Her entourage followed.

Bianca stared after them, her mouth gaping open stupidly. Hadn't the Duchess heard her? Hadn't she realised who she was? Could this be the same girl who'd laughed at the idea of wearing a snail-slime coloured dress, had run across the tiles with her skirts hitched around her legs, and yelled at the Baron when he displeased her?

Bianca felt a jabbing pain, as if the Duchess's indifference had stuck a sharp pin deep under her ribs. She scurried after them and reached out to touch the Duchess's sleeve. Part of her was vaguely horrified at her own bad manners, but she couldn't help it. 'Duchess, it's me. Bianca. Master di Lombardi's apprentice –'

'What do you think you're doing, peasant?' The Baron swatted her hand away. 'You've done quite enough damage for one day! Nobody may touch the Duchess of La Luminosa without my express permission!'

Your *permission?* Bianca thought, staring up at him,

111

then glancing at the Duchess again. Surely she wouldn't stand for him being so controlling?

They'd stopped walking, and Duchess Catriona turned to face Bianca. Bianca had hoped that she was just deep in thought, but there was no recognition in her eyes.

There was also something different about her face. Bianca frowned. When did the Duchess start wearing make-up to cover her birthmark? She had never seemed to mind it before.

Duchess Catriona looked at Bianca as if she didn't understand what she could possibly want, and then glanced at the Baron.

Bianca bit her lip to stop her jaw dropping open. Was Duchess Catriona looking to the Baron da Russo for instruction on what to say next?

'We are very sorry about Master di Lombardi,' said the Baron, as if he were being forced to form the words at knifepoint.

'Yes. Very sorry about Master di Lombardi,' said the Duchess. But she didn't seem sad. She didn't seem guilty, either. She just sounded . . . blank.

'I . . . thank you,' Bianca heard herself say, politeness apparently filling in when her brain was so shocked it could barely form a coherent thought.

The Baron and the Duchess turned to go. As they walked along the Gallery, their words echoed back to Bianca – mostly the Baron's words as he droned on, lecturing the Duchess on some subject that she would almost certainly have turned into a vigorous debate. But the Duchess was taking it in silently, with the occasional 'yes, Baron' or 'I see'.

She was being . . . *meek*.

'We'll make the announcement after the performance tonight,' said the Baron.

The Duchess simply nodded.

This is so wrong. I have to do something!

But what could she do? There was only one thing she could think of – one useful thing she could learn, despite the Duchess's state. She hurried along the Gallery, overtook Duchess Catriona again and stood in front of her, forcing her to stop. The Baron's face went as pink as one of the Maiden's Blush roses in the hothouse, but Bianca spoke before he could stop her.

'Your Highness, please, I need to ask you – you remember the other night, at the first night of your Ascension festivities? Master di Lombardi was there, unveiling the new picture of the White Tower. I . . . I think that you sent him a bottle –'

'How dare you, girl?' growled the Baron. He was bright red now – more like a Dragon's Blood rose than a Maiden's Blush – and his cheeks were quivering with anger. He looked like a steamcart engine overheating. 'I ought to throw you into the dungeons for this impudence!'

'Please, Your Highness!' Bianca begged. 'You must remember me.'

Duchess Catriona gave Bianca a long, quiet look. Then she turned to the Baron.

'Do you know this person, Duchess?' the Baron asked

113

her, his voice slow and even now. 'Is she bothering you? Shall I send her away?'

'Yes. Send her away,' said Duchess Catriona.

Bianca's heart sank like a stone.

'Guard!' the Baron yelled. 'Remove this girl! She is not to be allowed into the Duchess's sight again, understand?'

Bianca shuddered as the Guard seized her shoulder. The metal plates sewn to his heavy leather gloves dug into her skin. She tried to look up and meet the guard's eyes as he marched her out of the door, but his face was almost as blank as the Duchess's. It was obviously no use appealing to his sense of justice – or trying to convince him that there was something bad going on.

He steered her silently down the stairs and through the back corridors until they came to the back door to the servants' quarters. There, he opened the door and put her outside with a firm, but not unkind shove, as if she were a stray cat that'd been found in the larder licking the cream jug. The door slammed behind her and a bolt was drawn across.

Bianca folded her arms against her chest and shivered with a chill that had nothing to do with the weather.

Chapter Fourteen

Bianca stared through the darkness at the hands of the clock as it ticked slowly, unstoppably on towards the time of the troupe's performance for the Duchess. The rest of the girls in the dormitory at Filpepi's house were already in bed, breathing evenly. She had to get back into the palace tonight. She just needed to think of a plan.

Bianca twisted Duchess Catriona's handkerchief around her fingers. It had got her into the party on the first night, with its sun emblem and Catriona's initial, but would it work again tonight? And even if it did, she'd look as conspicuous as a gondola on the ocean if she turned up dressed like an artist's apprentice.

Bianca got up, treading silently across the wooden floor, and pulled open the drawer where her and Rosa's clothes were kept. It wasn't particularly encouraging. Rosa's dresses were nicer than hers, but far too big. Bianca's best dress was better than her worst dress, but it was certainly not a disguise. This time, it was more than chores and her master's disapproval on the line if she was caught. If the Baron saw her, he could throw her in the dungeon . . . or worse.

She shuddered, remembering some of the harsh judgements that had been handed out during the Baron's Regency. The urchins in the Piazza del Fiero sometimes told horror stories about children who'd been caught stealing and lost their hands, old men who'd criticised the Baron one day and never been seen again. She wasn't sure if any of the stories were true, but she didn't want to find out.

She needed nobody to doubt that she belonged at the ball. She needed a *proper* disguise. A costume . . .

Wait! Bianca could hear her blood beating in her ears. There were costumes. Plenty of costumes, right downstairs!

She crept for the door.

'Hey,' said Gabriella's sleepy voice from the mattress on the floor. Bianca cringed and froze. 'What're you doing? Running away?'

Bianca held her breath, trying to decide whether it'd be more suspicious if she just walked out. Even in her sleep, Gabriella was horrible . . .

'Oh shut up, Gabby,' said another sleepy voice from an upper bunk. It was Francesca. 'Go to sleep and leave her alone.'

Gabriella muttered something under her breath, turned over and pulled the covers up over her head.

Bianca's heart soared. Francesca presumably had no idea what she'd just done, but Bianca made a silent promise that one day she'd repay her. She snuck out of the room, holding the door so it made no sound as she swung it shut.

Filpepi's household seemed even bigger at night, when only the dim night-lamps were lit. Bianca ran as quietly as she could between the dancing ethereal shadows cast from the lights inside the paintings on the walls, and slipped quietly into the studio.

The costume cupboard was unlocked. Bianca grinned as she walked inside and found herself surrounded by clothes – coats and tunics, peasant rags, suits of armour, and a wide selection of ballgowns in every colour and size. She pushed away the belts and bells she'd been forced to wear the day before in favour of a rich-looking blue dress. It wasn't exactly the finest silk, but hopefully nobody would notice that. She picked out a light blue fan to go with it and pulled the dress on over her ordinary work dress.

She glanced in the mirror and held up the fan over her face. Would this get her past the guards? Perhaps, if they didn't look too closely.

In the distance, the bells in the chapels started to ring out over the city. It was too late to change her mind now. Either this would work, or . . . well, she'd think of something else later. Perhaps she could swim in through the Great Canal . . .

Bianca's two skirts bunched and rustled strangely as she slipped out of the studio and made a break for the front door. She put out her hand and closed it on the handle –

'What on earth do you think you are doing?'

Bianca winced at the volume of the voice behind her. It was Lucia. Bianca turned back to see Filpepi's head apprentice marching towards her, one hand out to grab at her sleeve.

'Take that off!' Lucia snapped. 'It doesn't belong to you!'

'I can't,' Bianca groaned. 'I know you don't understand, but I can't!'

'Don't be so stupid.' Lucia made a grab for her arm but Bianca twisted away.

'It's very important, I have to go, I'm sorry,' Bianca said, and threw open the front door. She hitched up her skirts and launched herself down the front steps and out into the shadows of the orange trees. She heard Lucia's footsteps behind her, but Bianca put on a burst of speed and turned sharp left, sprinting along the side of the dark canal.

'I won't allow this! I won't! Thief!' she heard Lucia shout after her, but her voice was getting dimmer. She wasn't following.

Bianca let herself stop to cool down for a moment when she reached the edge of the crowd waiting to cross over the Grand Canal into the palace. From the looks of things, the third night of the Duchess's Ascension festivities was just as lavish as the first ball Bianca had attended. If anything, the bridge was even more crowded with nobles making their way to see the play.

Bianca let herself be swept slowly along through the crowd towards the entrance to the palace and tried to hold her head up high, resisting the urge to fiddle with the white lace around her throat and her wrists. The dress fitted pretty well, except that she was quickly learning that this much deep blue silk and satin was *really* heavy. Bianca had never worn anything with this many layers. No wonder proper ladies needed maids to help them get dressed in the morning. She was pretty sure something somewhere wasn't buttoned right.

She peered between the shoulders of the glittering crowd and tried to make out the faces of the guards on the palace gate. If they knew her, she'd be in trouble. But she couldn't ignore the thought that even if they didn't, they might want to know why a girl with so many fake diamonds on her bodice was attending the ball alone, with only a mono-grammed handkerchief as an invitation.

A couple of steps in front of her there was a family with three daughters, all of whom had just the same deep brown-black hair as Bianca – though theirs was shinier and had seen a brush more recently.

Bianca smiled to herself as a plan sketched itself out in her mind.

She pulled out her fan and opened it so it covered most of her face, then took a few steps forward so she was walking close behind the three girls. They were talking excitedly about the feast and the play and the friends they were going to meet inside, and didn't notice that they had suddenly gained a scruffy, shy little sister.

The group drew up to the guards, and the mother pulled out their invitation from a glittering satin bag. The guard squinted at it. Bianca tensed, ready to run if this all went wrong.

'Lord and Lady Lutez and daughters,' said the guard. Lord Lutez gestured vaguely behind him, without looking. The movement encompassed the three chattering girls . . . and Bianca. 'Thank you,' said the guard, and waved them all through.

Bianca let out a long, slow breath as she walked inside. Her heart started to climb down from its position in the middle of her throat.

She was glad of her unknowing escort, because this celebration seemed very different from the one she'd been to before. There was no dancing in the courtyard, just a small string orchestra playing a slow sarabande. Inside the ballroom, instead of a milling crowd of people watching tumblers, and entertainers weaving between them, there were rows and rows of cushioned chairs facing a raised stage.

Duchess Catriona was already there, sitting at the side of the stage, with Baron da Russo to her left. He was still talking at her, and she was still staring into space, her face blank. Either she was listening intently to him, or she was ignoring him altogether. It had to be the second, Bianca thought. The Duchess had never listened to the Baron before.

Well, this is good, Bianca thought, finally splitting away from the three girls as the family struggled to find five seats together. *I'll be able to see the play . . . and the Duchess's reaction. Then I might be closer to unravelling my master's murder.*

She picked a seat at the back of the audience, next to an elderly noble lady who was watching through a pair of magnifying goggles on the end of a silver stick.

The lights in the ballroom suddenly dimmed, and Bianca caught her breath. This was it. The performance was about to begin . . .

A group of tumblers rolled onstage and immediately started a comic fight. She spotted Marco in the middle of the group, wearing his full costume make-up. The audience laughed as the characters tripped on their own swords, punched their friends by mistake, fell down and knocked themselves out on the scenery. Bianca laughed along with the rest, but then gasped.

The man who came on stage and began to speak was dressed as a king, in a flowing fur-lined cape, but he had a long white beard and walked with his neck pushed forward, like a turtle – just like di Lombardi. Was this intentional? Was this Marco's way of telling her the plan was going ahead?

Bianca's view of the play blurred, and for a while she couldn't concentrate on what was going on on the stage. Her mind was playing a different scene in front of her eyes. Her master, dressed in his finest, trailed around this very room by admirers and enthusiasts. Taking the wine from Marco. Seeing that she were there, and glaring at her . . .

Bianca would give anything if only he could glare at her like that again. If only she could stop seeing his face in front of her, as if she were back there, watching the curtain being pulled away from the new painting, watching the light flood the room, the surprise on her master's face, the appearance of the Duchess, and then the sudden fit of coughing . . .

'Drink this, my Lord,' said a voice, and the audience gasped. Bianca's attention snapped back to the stage. A girl in a ballgown was holding an oversized golden goblet up to the king. She had a glittering tiara perched on top of a long, flame-red wig.

'Dearest Princess, thank you. It is my favourite.' Bianca clutched the arms of her chair as the king drank deeply from the cup.

It's only a play, she told herself. *You can't bring him back by stopping the play.*

Her gaze found Duchess Catriona's face and fixed there, while the king handed the cup back to the princess. The Duchess's face was stony and blank. Was that a sign of fear? Of guilt? Maybe she didn't realise what was happening.

Or maybe the Duchess is the best actor in the room?

The actor playing the king had drawn his sword now, and he was facing up against a young lord in a fancy tunic and red-striped tights, who flourished his stage blade, forming a figure of eight in the air. The king took a step forward. The lord did too. The lord struck first, and the king easily parried the blow – and then he choked, doubled up, clutched his chest, and fell to the floor.

A doctor character in an enormously oversized black

hat and a long pointed mask like a bird's beak knelt by his side and pronounced him dead – 'Poisoned!' he shouted to the audience.

The Duchess's face hadn't changed the whole time. In fact, her eyes hadn't even moved to follow the action on the stage. Bianca felt sick.

She isn't watching. She's just staring into space. All this was for nothing. What is wrong with her?

The bad princess and her fancy lord embraced, and a chorus of weeping townsfolk came on stage to lament the end of the tragedy. The audience applauded and wiped their eyes, and the actors swept off their hats and wigs to take a bow. The Duchess didn't move, except to bring her hands together for a few seconds. Bianca didn't think you could actually call it applauding. Her hands barely touched.

Bianca caught Marco's eyes, and he widened them dramatically. He'd seen it too. Behind their bright actor-smiles, the whole troupe looked a bit haunted, as if each one of them feared for their lives, or at least their livelihoods.

The Duchess and Baron da Russo both got to their feet, and the guests fell silent as they walked up onto the stage. The actors crowded to one side to give them space. Bianca saw Marco's father steering him to his place with a quick squeeze of his shoulders. Master Xavier looked the most worried of all. His knuckles were white where they clutched his red-and-white staff.

The Baron da Russo swept a low, theatrical bow to

Master Xavier and the players, and then turned to face the audience with a wide smile on his round red face.

'My Lords, Ladies and Gentlemen,' said Baron da Russo, 'Thank you all for attending our dear Duchess Catriona's coming-of-age celebrations. Tomorrow is the last day of the festivities, her fourteenth birthday. By the end of the day she is to be crowned and will finally ascend to her full power as the Duchess of La Luminosa.'

There was enthusiastic applause from the audience. Bianca's hands clenched on her chair again. They were applauding the Duchess she used to know. Not this vague, unkind girl who stood meekly beside the Baron as he went on.

'I have acted as her Regent since her poor father, the Duke's, untimely death, and I hope that I have served the city well and fairly.'

There was more applause – but it was rather muted.

'But now, Duchess Catriona has become a woman – a beautiful, grown woman, with the wit and kindness to match. I have known our beloved Duchess her whole life, acted as her protector, friend and counsel through the years. Now . . .' he folded his hands in front of his chest. 'I am able to tell you all, dearest friends, of the feelings that have stirred in my heart. Our bond of guardianship has grown into something stronger, something even more wonderful.'

Bianca shuddered, as if a spider was crawling over her shoulders. What was this? What was he saying? It couldn't be . . .

'And I am incredibly proud and humbled to announce that our beautiful Duchess has consented to be my bride.'

For a moment Bianca wondered if this was one of her vivid dreams. There was no applause, only a shocked silence.

'We are to wed tomorrow in our private chapel, just before the coronation,' the Baron continued, a smug smile on his face. 'Afterwards we'll take the throne together as husband and wife.'

Bianca felt like someone had dropped a bucket of cold water down the back of her dress. The old lady sitting next to Bianca actually choked out a 'No!', before her adult son hurriedly shushed her. Then, slowly, the guests began to clap and cheer, crying out their congratulations to the happy couple.

And still, Duchess Catriona didn't smile, didn't look sad – didn't look like she was even in the room.

The crowd around her rose to their feet, still clapping, but to Bianca it all seemed to be happening in slow motion. The Duchess didn't even like the Baron – *nobody* liked the Baron. They weren't touching – not even holding hands. The Duchess's face was not the face of a girl who'd set her whole heart on marrying the man beside her.

Bianca stumbled to her feet, still staring at the Baron, and just for a second his roving, happy eyes landed on her and his expression darkened. Bianca gasped and threw her fan up over her face, but the Baron was already beckoning one of the guards.

He'd seen her.

Bianca turned and ran out of the ballroom, feeling like she was going to be sick. She had to lose them quickly, and get back to the Rose Gallery to meet Marco. This was clearly just the start of the Baron's evil plot. Something had to be done to protect the Duchess.

Chapter Fifteen

Bianca made it to the Rose Gallery before Marco. She was still panting from her flight, the two dresses she was wearing tugging at her skin and making her sweat, but she couldn't hear anyone following. She hoped maybe the guards wouldn't realise that she knew her way around this place, or wouldn't think she'd head for a deserted, half-finished corridor, but she crouched behind the door leading into the gallery, just in case. She'd hear them coming before they saw her.

The painting made the cool night-time hallway seem like it opened onto a magical world of constant warmth and daylight. Nobody had bothered to clear up the stool with her paints, though someone had shoved her leather toolbag aside and half of it was now inside the painting, between the rows of rose beds.

Marco arrived at a run, red face-paint still smudged across his cheek and between his eyebrows, and Bianca pulled him down beside her.

'What on earth?' he whispered, throwing his arms wide.

'I have no idea,' Bianca murmured back. 'Listen, I think the Baron saw me, we might not have long. There's no way the Duchess would marry him of her own accord. I don't know what he's done to her!'

'Right! I mean, she's only fourteen, and he's sixty if he's a day!'

'Maybe the Baron's drugged her,' Bianca said. 'Do you think there's a poison that can do that? Make someone all blank and obedient?'

Marco looked queasy. 'I hope not.' He folded himself up on the floor with his arms around his knees.

Bianca sighed. 'Were you watching her? It was like she wasn't even there.'

'Nobody in the audience looked like they noticed, either,' Marco grumbled. 'Maybe it was too subtle. Like you said – that sort of thing always happens in plays.'

'Well, thank you for trying,' Bianca said miserably. She sat beside him on the floor with her back to the window, staring up at the artificial light from the artificial hothouse.

'I don't see how you do it,' Marco said, gesturing to the painting. 'Make light like that. You must be magic.'

'I don't really know how I do it,' Bianca confessed. 'But I don't know how you jump as far as you do or swing off those high ropes.'

Marco shuddered. 'I'm not so sure about the ropes any more, after that stunt on the burning roof. I think I'd rather keep my feet on the ground for a bit.' He was still staring at the painting, and his face slowly formed into a frown. 'It's like the one Master di Lombardi painted for the Duchess. The picture of the room in the White Tower.'

'Except it won't be as good,' Bianca corrected him hurriedly. She looked again at the painting and instantly disliked it. 'I can see so many mistakes I need to redo. I have to finish this one by myself, and Master di Lombardi was the only person who worked on the coronation gift. I'd never even seen it till . . . that night.'

'Hmm,' said Marco, and then fell silent. Bianca glanced at him. He was frowning, and raised his hand to wipe at the make-up streaked on his cheek.

'What're you thinking?' Bianca asked. Maybe it wasn't the Duchess who gave him the wine, or he'd remembered the Baron da Russo giving it to her first . . . that would make all of this much simpler.

'It's just . . . didn't he make a face, right before he . . . before he fell down? Like he was surprised?'

'Well, yes. It was because the Duchess was there after all, and we'd been told she wasn't coming.'

'Was it?' Marco shut his eyes and pinched the bridge of his nose. 'Think back. *Really* think. Was it when the Duchess came in? Or was it when he unveiled the painting?'

Bianca thought hard.

The velvet curtain fell away from the painting, and light flooded the room . . . the crowd sighed . . . Bianca's head whipped around to see Duchess Catriona at the back of the room with the Baron da Russo . . . Master di Lombardi gasped, but he was looking from the painting to the Duchess and back to the painting, as if something wasn't right . . .

'You . . . you think there was something wrong with the painting?' Bianca asked.

'Maybe someone had added something to it,' Marco replied. 'Or changed it in some way. I don't know, but it looked to me like there was something about the painting he wasn't expecting.'

'I . . . I think you're right.' As soon as she'd said it, she was sure. Marco *was* right. 'But I don't know how we can tell. *Nobody* saw the painting before except my master. He always snuck off to some secret studio to work on it. I mean, I've never even seen the cartoons – they weren't found when we were cleaning up the studio. Master Filpepi's still looking for the last of the sketchbooks. They probably burned up in the fire. Although . . .'

There were the other notebooks. And the passage to the church. What if there's yet more secret hiding places in the old house that I just haven't found yet?

Marco groaned and dropped his head onto his knees.

Bianca's hand strayed to the large purse tied at her waist. 'I did find something, when I went back. I found a secret chamber where he kept some of his notebooks. But none of them are to do with the Ascension painting. They're pretty odd. I don't see how they could help.' She untied the string from the bag, pulled out the small, leathery notebook and passed it to Marco. 'I've been carrying it around with me,' she admitted, when he raised his eyebrows at her. 'I like having something of his.'

Marco took the notebook and flipped through it. 'I don't know what half this stuff is supposed to be,' he said.

130

'Did he really try to make these? Harpsichords that play themselves? I mean, a *flying* machine?'

'He tinkered with them, I think,' Bianca said. 'He made little models sometimes. He always said they were the foolish dreams of an old man.'

'Maybe there is a clue in here,' said Marco, 'or in the sketches for the Duchess's painting. You said Filpepi was looking for them, maybe he's suspicious too.'

Bianca hadn't thought of that. Could Master Filpepi be investigating di Lombardi's death? Marco went on looking through the notebook, and she got to her feet and brushed herself down.

'We've got to find a way out of the palace,' she said. But the only way out was past the guards at the front door. She searched around the room for a disguise – *anything* – some kind of inspiration for how to escape.

Her gaze fell back to the painting that she'd been working on that afternoon. It was looking much better than when she'd begun, but it wouldn't pass for a di Lombardi painting. It wouldn't even pass for a Filpepi in this state. She needed to add a bush or two to the scene that was visible through the glass, so that it looked like there was a real world on the other side, and the glass itself was a bit suspiciously clear – not warped like real glass would be. And it wouldn't hurt to add a lot more shine to this handle . . .

In fact, she could see, suddenly, that if she put a little bit of shine *here* and *here* and she darkened the space under the handle, it would feel a lot more solid . . .

Bianca picked up her paintbrush. Maybe this could be a way out.

Marco said something, but she only heard it as a murmur at the edge of her hearing, like a fly buzzing in the room.

. . . this shadow needed to be a lot darker, and much bluer. A lot of apprentices were afraid of colour, they thought that splashing blue around in their shadows would make things look unrealistic – but real shadows *were* blue, and sometimes wood was red and skin was green.

She reached out, her brush ready to add a last touch to the edge of the handle, but her eyesight tricked her and she missed. Her fingers touched something cold and solid. She gasped.

The handle was real! She ran a finger along its length, where there should have been wet paint, but only felt cool metal.

'I've done it,' she whispered.

'What?' Marco stood up and came to stand beside her.

'Touch that handle.'

'I can't,' said Marco. 'I mean I know it looks like I can, but it's just a trick, right?'

'Master di Lombardi's been teaching me,' Bianca said, mostly to herself. 'But I've never got it right. I've never made it work. Until now . . .'

She put her hand up and touched the glass in the door. It felt like glass. The wood and copper frame felt like wood and copper, slightly warm under the fake sunlight streaming in through the fake windows. Instead of just being painted to *look* like a whole door, it *was* a whole door. This was so much more than a jumping stick figure.

Marco gingerly put out a hand out and touched the handle, and then yelped. 'It's metal!'

'I know! I've done it! I've mastered the technique!' Excitement and happiness swelled up in Bianca until she couldn't help but jump up on the spot, hugging her paintbrush in a happy little dance. Marco took a step back, laughing at her. Bianca stopped dancing and brushed her hair out of her eyes. 'I can *make* things, real things! This is incredible! Master di Lombardi would have been so . . .' she broke off, smiling. 'I'm sorry, what were you saying? You said something. I wasn't paying attention because *I can paint things into being!*'

Marco laughed again. 'I can see how that would be distracting,' he grinned. 'I was just reading something from the notebook. It's weird. It was written on the back page, but I didn't get it until I blurred my eyes. Look . . .' He held out the notebook. 'Can you see it?'

Bianca looked at the page. She wasn't sure she would've guessed that the scrawl on the back page was even supposed to be words – they seemed to be random shapes, semi-circles and little dashes and odd squiggles. Some of them were overlaid on top of each other.

'You have to try to focus your eyes on the other side of the page, so it blurs,' said Marco.

Bianca gasped. She unfocused her eyes, until there were two of the page swimming in front of her, and suddenly the squiggles and dashes lined up and formed six words.

'It says *hidden rooms, secret passages, second city*,' said Marco. 'Sounds like nonsense to me. But why would he write it in code?'

For a second, the words seemed to echo around Bianca's mind. She knew she'd heard them before. She was sure of it. *Protect the Duchess.*

'I think Master di Lombardi tried to tell me that,' she muttered. 'Just after he collapsed at the ball, he said . . .' she put her hand on the handle of the door, feeling its brand new reassuring coolness under her palm. 'Hidden rooms,' she muttered. 'Secret passages. Second city.'

There was a sound, like tiny clockwork parts winding down. Bianca jumped. The paintbrush was vibrating gently as it dangled in her fingers. She held it out, cradling it gingerly in her palms. The handle split neatly along a break in the wood that she'd never seen before. About a third of its length slid aside and tucked itself away inside the hollow cavity that opened up. Bianca could just make out whirring cogs, but so tiny that they must've been painted in with a single hair. Then a set of copper prongs unfolded out of the hole, clicking into place. The top of the paintbrush handle became, unmistakably, a key.

The whirring noises stopped. Bianca stared at the key in her hand for a moment.

'Try it!' Marco whispered. 'Go on. Try it in the door!'

Bianca swallowed. 'Just . . . give me a minute.'

The silence filled with footsteps. Voices echoed down the corridor, coming towards them. Bianca recognized that droning sound. The Baron! He'd fetched Filpepi too!

'You haven't got a minute,' hissed Marco.

She leapt forward, right into the painting, her feet landing on the unfinished painted wooden floor with a slightly canvassy thud, thrust the key into the keyhole and turned it.

Marco grabbed the handle and the door swung open; not onto the scene that Bianca had painted onto its glass window, but onto a long, dim corridor of dark stone, the walls spattered with a constellation of glittering colour.

The voices were nearly on them. Bianca grabbed the toolbag and ran inside, pushing Marco in front of her. It was just like the passage that Master di Lombardi had taken them through during the fire. The same walls, the same stone, even the same smell. Bianca quickly closed the door behind them. They were safe inside the secret passage. And now Bianca knew how to create them.

Chapter Sixteen

Bianca stared, stunned, back through the glass window in the door. She could see the hothouse, with its rainbow of rose beds and ochre tiles on the floor, but when she looked to her right, she could see out of the painting into the Rose Gallery, with its real walls and floors and windows.

'I can't believe I did this,' she whispered. Was it di Lombardi's years of training that had suddenly paid off . . . or had Filpepi's extra tuition had something to do with it? Either way, she felt very proud of herself.

She ducked back, hiding behind the doorframe, as Baron da Russo and Master Filpepi strolled into view. Filpepi glanced at the painting, but he was looking at the roses, and he looked away quickly. She heard a snatch of conversation:

'. . . nearly ready.'

'The wedding is tomorrow, everything needs to be perfect . . .'

And then the two men had reached the other end of the Gallery and disappeared through the door.

She turned to look at Marco, who was staring around at the secret passage with his jaw hanging open.

'How can this passage be here?' he said. 'It's the same place we came into from your house, in the fire! It has to be.'

Bianca looked down at the paintbrush-key. The thing her master had taken from her pocket, the thing he'd dropped on the floor in the church – it *had* been the paintbrush, after all. It all made sense. The paintbrush was also a key.

Marco was still frowning. 'How can there be a passage that goes all the way from the palace to the middle of the city, but nobody knows about it?'

'And the Rose Gallery's on the second floor,' Bianca pointed out. 'But I don't see any steps or ramps'. She ran her fingers over the dark stone walls, touching a few splatters of paint and one of the flickering candles in its brass holder. 'I think this place isn't . . . *real*. Not in the same way as the city's real, anyway.'

'But we're standing in it,' said Marco.

'You can stand in paintings, too, remember?' She looked around again, then walked up to the wall and touched it. It felt like stone, but there was that smell again – the smell of paint and canvas. 'It's like di Lombardi painted himself an entire world.'

'Do you think this is what "second city" means?'

'I suppose it must be,' said Bianca.

They started to walk forward, into the dark passage. It wasn't long before they came to another door. This one was plain wood, but it too had a little window just at head-height. Bianca stood on tiptoes and looked through it.

'It's another painting,' she said. 'Look, there's Santa Juanita in her armour by the painted altar over there, but you can see the real altar at the other end of the church. We're inside the trompe l'oeil that Master di Lombardi painted in the Duchess's private chapel!'

Marco looked through the window and whistled through his teeth.

'There's no way we've walked as far as the chapel. This is so strange . . .'

'Of course. It's like this is a shortcut between each of the paintings in the palace. Maybe between every painting Master di Lombardi ever painted! Anywhere in the city!'

Marco jogged over to the next door and peered through the keyhole. 'I can see gauzy curtains, and a tree in a pot, and a little chair . . . this is the Duchess's private chambers.'

Bianca looked too. The Duchess wasn't there, but there were two maids in the room. One was sweeping the ochre tiles, while the other sat on the Duchess's couch, with her feet up. 'Cheeky!' Bianca grinned. 'She's going to be in trouble if the Baron catches her.'

Marco leaned over and rapped sharply on the door. Bianca saw the maid jump off the couch as if it were on fire, look around guiltily, fail to find the source of the noise and then go back to sweeping.

Bianca couldn't help laughing at the maid's panicked face. 'Oh, that was mean,' she said to Marco.

The next door was a rickety old thing made of warped planks of wood nailed haphazardly together. Light spilled into the dim passage through its many cracks. Bianca put her eye to one of the holes, and Marco joined her at another, and then gasped.

'Father!'

Marco's father, Master Xavier, was standing in the room on the other side of the painting, packing props and costumes away in a large trunk.

'This is the painting of the old overgrown garden,' Marco whispered. 'It's on the wall in our dressing room!'

Master Xavier turned to the lady tumbler who'd been the princess in the play. She was untangling her black hair from the long wig. 'Where has that boy got to, Ophelia?' he said.

'Marco? I haven't seen him since the curtain. He'll be fine.'

'As long as he's not getting into trouble,' Master Xavier sighed. 'I don't know, we're out of favour with the Duchess for some reason, and now the Baron's taking back power . . . I think it'd be best if we moved on as soon as the wedding's over.'

Ophelia shook her head. 'There'll never be a gig like this again. We'll be playing little market town squares for the rest of our lives.'

'I don't know. Perhaps we could take a ship across the Caspar, try our luck at the Tsarina's court. Either way, better to live long, poor lives doing what we love than outstay our welcome here and end up in the Baron's dungeons.'

Ophelia nodded sadly.

Bianca glanced at Marco.

'Father's right,' he muttered, pulling away from the door. 'It's not fair, but it's true. If we can't get good work here, we have to move on.'

Bianca really wished he was wrong. Rosa and the rest of di Lombardi's apprentices felt like good friends – not quite family, but close enough – but she couldn't expose them to danger by telling them the secret of di Lombardi's death. What would she do if the only other person who knew the truth about her master's murder had to leave the city?

The next door showed them the Duchess's bedroom. Bianca knew it at once, because she had gone inside to fetch a shawl for the Duchess once. It was a large room with plush red rugs on the floor, an enormous bed, huge oak wardrobes and a reclining couch. The painting they were looking through was of a cozy night-time hearth. Bianca squinted as she peered through the window in the door. The candles and lamps were all out, even the night-lamp, and the room was lit only by the dim flickering of the painted fire. Nothing inside moved. Bianca was about to look away and tell Marco it was empty . . . then the dancing shadows flickered over a face.

Bianca yelped and clamped her hands over her mouth.

Duchess Catriona was sitting up in bed, so still Bianca couldn't see her breathing. She was staring straight in front of her, not even blinking.

'That's so creepy,' Bianca whispered, letting Marco look. Marco shuddered and nodded.

'Who just stares into space like that?' he murmured. 'I used to know a ventriloquist – he could make it look like his doll was talking and he wasn't. She looks like that!'

It was a chilling thought. Bianca couldn't imagine that the Duchess would ever choose to marry the Baron if she was still in control of her life. So what had he done? Given her some concoction to make her placid? Or was he blackmailing her? Had he killed di Lombardi as part of this plan – or was he using the knowledge that she'd had the great artist murdered to manipulate her?

Or was it something even more sinister . . .?

Bianca wrapped her arms around herself and quickly drew away from the room. 'Let's go. I can't bear to watch her like this.'

They came to a crossroads, and went straight on, though Bianca could see that the passages they didn't take also went on and on into the distance, studded with doors on both sides.

'I bet you could get anywhere in the city from here,' said Marco. 'I suppose if we knew the way we could find our way back to di Lombardi's house, or to Santa Cecilia's.'

'Not the house – the painting the door was in burned up. It doesn't exist any more. But look! This is even better!' Bianca said, looking through a small window in a door that seemed carved out of stone. 'This painting is in Filpepi's study.'

She slipped the key into the door and unlocked it.

The study was nearly as dark as the Duchess's bedroom. The heavy curtains had been drawn, shutting out any moonlight. There was a lamp still burning on the desk, but it had been covered with a green and blue silk scarf. It cast rippling blue-green lines of light around the room. Bianca thought the effect was rather as if they were walking around under the water of one of the canals.

Marco stumbled as he stepped out of the painting and waved his hands in front of his face.

'How can you just walk around in this darkness? I can't see a thing! Why hasn't the maid lit his night-lamp?'

'It's not *that* dark. There's still a light, look, on the desk.'

Marco squinted. 'There's *something* glowing, there, but I can't see that it's a lamp – ow,' he complained.

'Careful!' Bianca reached out to steady him. 'There's an easel right in front of you. This way.' She steered him around the easel with its big canvas, which faced away from them towards the desk. It must be the painting of the Grand Duchess Angelica in her wedding dress, which Filpepi had been restoring. Bianca wondered if he'd somehow known before everyone else that the Duchess was going to marry the Baron. Maybe it was supposed to be a wedding gift . . .

'All right, you can let go, I can see now,' said Marco. 'Aah!' He yelped and grabbed Bianca's arm again.

'What? What?' Bianca gasped.

'Oh thank god – I thought that dress was a person,' Marco explained, pointing to a drooping shape. 'It's so sparkly I thought it was moving.'

Bianca looked where Marco was pointing, and gasped. 'It's the dress! The Grand Duchess Angelica's wedding dress.' It hung by the door, placed on a hook. But with the amount of underskirts the dress had, it could have stood up on its own. 'At least, it must be a replica.' Bianca went over to the desk and carefully lifted the scarf from the lamp. The light fell on the dress and the room filled with tiny points of light, reflecting from every surface of every one of the diamonds. Bianca blinked and rubbed her eyes, dazzled by the glare. Marco stared at the dress, wide-eyed.

'But . . . why is it here?' Bianca frowned, staring at the beautiful dress. 'I was working on the painting . . . this morning.' It felt odd that it was only this morning that she was working happily under Filpepi's tutelage. 'If Master Filpepi's using this dress to help him restore the painting, why didn't he show me?'

'Could it –'

Suddenly there was a hard rap on the door. Bianca jumped and let the scarf fall back across the lamp, putting out the dancing specks of light.

'What's going on in there? Who is it?'

Bianca drew in a breath. That was Cosimo's voice.

'Is that you, Bianca?' Cosimo rattled the door handle, but it was locked. 'Unlock this door and come out, right now!'

Bianca and Marco looked at each other, and then looked back at the painting of an ancient ruined chapel that they'd walked out of.

'We could go back in, find another way . . .' Marco suggested in a whisper.

Bianca shook her head. 'No, I'd better face him.' She pulled the paintbrush key from her pocket and unlocked the door, then hid the key behind her back as the door flew open and Cosimo half-fell inside.

He glared at Bianca, and glared even harder at Marco. 'Bianca!' he gasped. 'Sneaking around Master Filpepi's private studio, in the middle of the night, *with a strange boy* . . . what on earth are you doing?' Bianca bit her lip, letting his fury wash over her. 'I thought you were a burglar! How did you get the key to his study? And who is this?'

'I'm terribly sorry,' said Marco smoothly, his voice changed. 'Let me introduce myself.' He held a hand out to Cosimo and smiled. Bianca stared at him. 'My name is Marco Xavier. I met Bianca at the palace, and I'm such an enthusiast, you know, I'm afraid I just insisted that she bring me back to the studio for a tour. Please don't punish her – you can write to my father about my behaviour, if you would like.'

Bianca's jaw fell open, but she quickly closed it. Marco had drawn his back up straight and was speaking in a precise manner, and that was all he needed to convince Cosimo he was some kind of young lord. He hadn't told a single lie, and Cosimo obviously bought it. Cosimo blinked at her for a second in a panicky kind of way, and then shook Marco's hand.

'Um. No, that's all right. I quite understand, Your Lordship. But Bianca, you shouldn't have shown him Filpepi's study,' he said to her. 'Why don't you let me show you the rest of the studio myself, Sir? Some of the artwork is available to buy, you know. If you see anything you like, do say.' He led Marco from the room and turned back to growl at Bianca. 'To bed. Now.'

Bianca nodded, and – still trying not to grin – dipped a little curtsey in Marco's direction.

'Perhaps I'll see you again,' Marco told her. 'Thank you for showing me the statue of the lion on the Palace Bridge, earlier. I might go and see it again at midday tomorrow.'

'Certainly, Sir, it's no trouble,' said Bianca, catching Marco's meaning. Then she fled for the girls' dormitory before the sight of Cosimo bowing low to Marco could make her break cover and burst into giggles.

Chapter Seventeen

'She's a thief! I'm telling you!'

Bianca snapped awake, her heart pounding before she realised why. Then she heard the raised voices. Outside the dormitory, climbing the stairs, coming nearer. She sat up, rubbed her eyes and ran her hands through her hair. Early morning light was streaming through the window.

'I don't need any wild accusations from you, Lucia,' said Filpepi's voice.

'But, Sir, Bianca stole –'

'I said that's enough!' Filpepi growled. 'Go in there and get them up.'

The dormitory door opened, hitting the wall with a bang. Lucia marched in.

'Everyone up!' she shouted. 'Quick, quick. Master Filpepi wants to talk to Bianca.' She gave Bianca a look with daggers in it. Bianca threw back the covers and tumbled out of bed and stood respectively. Lucia nudged Gabriella with her foot and dragged Francesca down from her bunk to stand beside Bianca. Rosa stared blearily at her.

'What is it?' she muttered. 'What's going on?'

'I need to speak to Bianca,' said Master Filpepi. He found her across the dormitory, his face a mask of fury. The other apprentices had climbed hastily out of bed and were standing to attention, looking from their Master to Bianca with wide eyes. Behind him in the corridor, Cosimo, Domenico and Sebastiano were hovering, watching the commotion but wary of stepping inside the girls' bed chamber.

Bianca felt her face going bright red. The distance from her bed to the doorway seemed like miles. Filpepi stood and waited, his arms folded and his foot tapping.

'Is it true?' he demanded. 'Were you thrown out of the palace yesterday?'

'Um . . .' Bianca swallowed. 'I . . . the Baron –'

'Not the Baron. *You*. Is it true that you *accosted* the Duchess? That you tried to seize her and hold her against her will?'

The other apprentices gasped. Bianca looked around at their shocked faces, trying to make eye-contact with Rosa and then with Domenico, to tell them it wasn't as bad as it sounded. But when Filpepi put it like that, it did sound pretty bad.

'I'm sorry,' she said, 'I . . . I needed to ask her something and I thought she just hadn't heard me, and –'

'Oh yes. The Baron told me about your questions. He said you demanded to know about her movements, and about her actions on the night of the first Ascension festivities.'

'Yes, because –'

'No, don't try to explain yourself.' Filpepi held up a hand. 'There is *no excuse* for this. How dare you interrogate Her Highness as if she were some common servant?'

Everyone was staring at Bianca. She opened and shut her mouth. She could explain everything, if he'd only give her the chance, but then again, where on earth could she start?

'And now Lucia tells me that you're a thief!' Filpepi growled. 'I demand that you tell me the truth, or so help me, I will expel you from my studio this very morning. Did you steal from me last night?'

Bianca took a deep breath. 'No,' she said. The lie came so much easier than her attempts to tell the truth, it was almost shocking. 'I was in bed. I didn't take anything. Lucia's mistaken.'

'Then what's *that*?' Lucia pointed, a look of horrible triumph on her face. Bianca turned to look. There was an unmistakeably dress-like corner of blue silk sticking out from under her bed. She swallowed hard, her heart sinking into her toes. She was so sure she'd hidden it deep underneath the bed before she went to sleep last night. She was such an idiot for not checking.

Lucia marched over and tugged on the silk. The dress came out in one heavy, crumpled rustle.

'Bianca, this will not stand,' said Filpepi. 'I have no choice –'

148

'Wait!' Francesca stepped forward, her whole small body trembling. 'It was me. I took the dress.'

Bianca was too shocked to speak.

'Francesca, stop lying to Master Filpepi,' Lucia hissed, 'Or you know it will be worse for you!'

'I just wanted to try on the costumes,' Francesca insisted bravely. 'I've always wanted to. I brought it up here to try on and I forgot to put it back. I'm so sorry.'

Bianca looked from Francesca's small, shamed-looking face up to Filpepi's furious one and back again. He couldn't punish Francesca too harshly, could he? If Bianca had done something like that, Master di Lombardi would have put her on washing-up duty for a month. Bianca could do that for Francesca.

'You'll have to leave,' said Filpepi. Francesca gasped. Bianca heard shocked mutters from the boys out in the hall. Even Lucia's face turned pale, though she fixed Francesca with an I-told-you-so look. 'I won't tolerate thievery, even from stupid little girls. If you took this without permission, you are dismissed.'

Francesca gulped and started to cry.

Bianca could not let this happen. 'I did it,' Bianca blurted out. 'Francesca's covering for me. I took the dress and snuck out to meet a friend.' Francesca gave her a pathetically grateful smile. Somehow, Bianca managed to smile back. She would take her punishment like an adult. 'I'm sorry,' she said, meekly, but raising her chin to meet Filpepi's eyes.

Filpepi shook his head. 'This is unacceptable behaviour,

Bianca. I won't have it in my house. Rosa, help Bianca pack her things and take her out.' Bianca shut her eyes. 'She doesn't work here any more. She doesn't live here any more.'

'But . . . But where will she go?' asked Francesca, her voice trembling.

'That is no longer our concern,' said Filpepi.

Bianca wanted to move, wanted to open her mouth and argue and plead for her position, but she felt as if someone had cast her in stone. She just stared at Filpepi so hard that, after a moment, he actually looked a little uncomfortable and looked away.

He walked out of the studio and left Bianca standing like a statue in a circle of shocked, staring faces.

She had a vague impression of people being kind to her, putting their hands on her shoulders and speaking to her in soft, encouraging voices. Rosa put a canvas bag into her hands – it didn't seem to weigh anything – and hugged her, leaving a soggy patch on the shoulder of her dress. Then she was walking out of Filpepi's house, and the door shut behind her. She stood under the orange trees and breathed in their sweet scent, dawn breezes stirring her hair. Within about five minutes, her whole life had turned upside down. She was just as alone as she had been when she'd been left on the doorstep of Master di Lombardi's house as a baby. She had no one, and nowhere to go. She had no apprenticeship, no job, no home.

If she wasn't an artist any more, what was she?

No. I am still an artist. I'll be an artist if I have to make a living drawing with chalk in the Piazza del Fiero and sleeping in the portico of Santa Cecilia's.

The thought cheered her, a little bit. She picked one of Filpepi's oranges, not caring that she could be plainly seen from the house and the street, and peeled it as she walked out of the drive and across the bridge.

Without anywhere to go, she wandered for hours, crossing bridges and ducking down alleys until she came to the side of the Canal Angelica, where the stone railings along the water were low enough for her to climb up and sit on.

All she possessed in the world was now in the canvas bag slung over her shoulder. She had never felt so alone – an orphan and a name unwelcome in any decent house. She only had one friend now: Marco.

Hang on! she thought. *Marco!*

She raced to their meeting place on the Palace Bridge.

Marco was waiting for her there, sitting with his back propped against the great stone lion that roared out over the Grand Canal towards the sea.

He shaded his eyes with one hand as Bianca approached.

'What's that?' he asked, with a nod at her bag.

Bianca dropped the bag by his side and sat down. 'I got sacked for sneaking out yesterday and trying to talk to Duchess Catriona. Please tell me you've found something out, because I don't think I'm going to be much help inside the palace from now on.'

Marco gaped at her for a second, and then a thoughtful

look came over his face. 'When you tried to speak to the Duchess, did she ignore you, or did she get cross?'

'She . . . actually, she didn't seem to know me. She wasn't particularly angry. Just confused.'

'Aha!' Marco smiled.

'What? *Aha* what?'

'Well . . . what if there's a simple reason for all of this? Why does the Duchess not seem like the Duchess? Why did she seem not to know you?' He paused for dramatic effect, but before he could go on, the answer hit Bianca like a thunderbolt striking the White Tower.

'Because she *doesn't* know me. And it *isn't* the Duchess!' She stared at Marco, who beamed back. 'But that's mad!' she said. 'How could the Baron have found an exact double? Does the Duchess have an identical twin?'

'Could be magic,' Marco shrugged. 'Maybe he's made some other girl look like the Duchess. I don't know. But he's done it somehow. Now all we need to do is prove it.'

Bianca stared at her hands for a while, trying to line up this new theory in her head. She'd never heard that the Baron dabbled in magic, but he was rich enough, and ambitious enough, to hire someone to do it for him. 'My poor master,' she said, after a moment's thought. 'I bet he worked it out and tried to stop the Baron. He told me to protect the Duchess. But I didn't know what to protect her from. And now it's too late. The Baron is going to marry her and steal back the throne.'

Marco stood up. He held out a hand and dragged Bianca to her feet. 'It's not too late if we can find the real

Duchess and expose the Baron. We have to get back into the palace and search the Duchess's rooms for clues.' Marco handed Bianca her bag. 'After all, if we can find the real Duchess, she'll be able to tell Filpepi you weren't rude to her, you were just trying to help, and he'll give you your apprenticeship back.'

'But there's no way I'll be let inside now,' Bianca said. 'I'm banned from the palace and the studio – from just about everywhere, actually,' she added. Her stomach rumbled and she flushed and wrapped her arms around herself. 'Just my luck to become homeless before breakfast,' she said.

Marco gave her a smile and a short bow. 'Then allow me to provide lunch. When I say me,' he added, as they walked down the bridge, 'I mean the San Franco Beneficent Society. But it's better than nothing, right?'

There was already a pretty long queue at the Francos' stall when Bianca and Marco arrived in the Piazza del Corvis. It was always busy around midday, as the city's poor and destitute converged on the square in search of a free charitable meal before they had to find shelter from the heat of the sun.

Bianca's heart sank as she joined the line behind an old man with one leg and one eye. She didn't want to be a beggar. But she supposed not one person in this line had ever *wanted* to be a beggar. She was back at the beginning of her life; homeless and without family. Perhaps this was her irrevocable destiny.

The monks serving the food were kindly old men in

scratchy-looking brown robes. She took a piece of stale bread and a cup full of thin broth, and went to sit and eat it on the steps of the church. It wasn't exactly Mistress Quinta's wonderful olive bread, but it was definitely food.

'Don't fuss now, Angela,' said a familiar voice.

Mistress Quinta?

Bianca looked up, searching the rag-tag crowd, and then gasped and almost dropped the last of her broth into her lap.

'Marco,' she said, tugging at his sleeve. 'Look! That's di Lombardi's housekeeper! And Angela, the kitchen girl!' She thrust the bowl of broth into his hands and stood up to run across the square. They both looked a mess – Angela's hair was knotted and she had a large bruise on her cheek, and Mistress Quinta's apron was covered in dirt and grime.

'Bianca!' Angela gasped when she saw her approach. Bianca ran up and grabbed Angela into a tight hug.

'What happened to you two?' Bianca asked them. 'Master Filpepi said –'

'Master Filpepi!' Mistress Quinta unceremoniously spat on the ground. 'There's for your *Master Filpepi*. We came to him to plead for our jobs and he turned us out, said there was nothing he could do for us. He wouldn't even give us references. We had to sleep on the street!'

'What? Why would he do that?' Bianca gasped. 'He told me he'd take care of you!'

'Well, then he lied,' said Mistress Quinta.

Bianca could not believe the tragedy after tragedy that

154

had taken place since di Lombardi's death. All this time she thought it was only her who had been affected. But it was Mistress Quinta, Angela, the Duchess, Marco's troupe . . . everyone.

'I'll fix this,' Bianca promised. 'I will.'

'How?' asked Angela quietly. 'Can you get us a new position?'

'I . . . I'll go back,' Bianca said. Marco gave her a surprised look but she squared her shoulders. 'Filpepi threw me out too, but I deserved it. You two have done nothing wrong! I'll go and try to talk to him for you.'

Angela threw her arms around Bianca again and Mistress Quinta pressed her hand tight.

'Bless you for trying, Bianca. Master di Lombardi would have been proud,' she said.

At the mention of her old master's name, Bianca's eyes started to well. She would make him proud. And she would right all the wrongs since his death, even if she ended up in jail for her efforts.

Chapter Eighteen

Bianca started to question her own judgment almost as soon as they'd left the Piazza del Corvis, but she couldn't turn back now.

Her spirits rose when she saw that a large, beautiful carriage decorated in black and bright blue was standing at the end of Filpepi's drive. Looking down the path through the orange trees, she saw Filpepi himself striding out of his house.

'You should hide,' she hissed to Marco. 'I don't want to have to explain you as well!' Marco nodded and nimbly climbed up into the branches of the nearest orange tree and froze, cleverly concealed among the fruit and leaves.

Bianca watched as Filpepi walked down the drive. He was dressed in a fine black jerkin embroidered with sparkling blue, like veins, or the sparks of lightning bolts, and he was pulling black gloves onto his hands.

Is he dressed for the wedding? Bianca wondered. *But that's not for hours.*

He didn't see her until he was almost right in front of her, but when he did he stopped and his brows drew down into a scowl that made Bianca think that maybe this talk was not going to go well.

'Master Filpepi, please may I speak to you?' she began.

'Get out of my way,' Filpepi snarled, and pushed past her. Bianca stared after him for a second in shock, but then her anger bubbled back to the surface and she chased after him.

'The wedding's not til this evening,' she said. 'I'm sure you have time to talk. It's not about me, it's about Mistress Quinta and –'

Filpepi turned on her, his nostrils flaring, and opened his mouth as if to yell – then looked up. Two ladies were passing the gate and had stopped to stare at them. Filpepi tensed and drew in a long breath. 'I have a special part in the wedding party,' he growled. 'Don't you *dare* try to hold me up.'

'But you said you'd help them!' Bianca insisted. She leapt in front of him, putting herself between him and the carriage. 'I'm not moving until you tell me why you threw them out! You promised you'd take care of them. You've been so kind to the apprentices –'

Filpepi laughed. He met the ladies' eyes and smiled handsomely at them. 'Oh I see. There's no need to worry at all, Bianca. It's a misunderstanding.'

The ladies smiled back and walked on. As soon as their backs were turned, though, Filpepi leaned in and turned his smile on Bianca . . . and it wasn't handsome or friendly

157

at all. He grabbed her arm and she yelped as his fingers dug into her.

'You have misunderstood me, girl,' he said, through a cold grin. 'Why should I be kind to you unless it suits me? Why should I take in all di Lombardi's waifs and strays just because the old fool is dead?'

Bianca gaped at him. 'You *lied* to us?'

'Only as long as it pleased me.'

'Ow!' Bianca tried to tear her arm out of his grip but he held on tight.

'You've all been useless,' Filpepi went on. 'Even his head apprentice didn't know enough of the old fool's techniques! You, though . . .' he gave Bianca another creepy smile. 'You were actually quite helpful. I should be thanking you. Though your friends may not, when they find they're all out on the street.'

'What? Why?' Bianca's head was spinning. She couldn't follow this. Filpepi had learned from *her*? Was that why he'd allowed her to work on the painting of the Grand Duchess – because he wanted to see what she would do? 'Why would you throw them all out, you need them!'

'Not after today,' said Filpepi. 'This wedding is going to change everything. And if you know what's good for you you'll stay out of my way until it's done.'

He pushed her, hard. She stumbled and hit the ground. Her hands and knees stung as they slammed into the pavement. She looked up to yell at him, but was just in time to see him climb into the waiting carriage.

'You fraudster!' she shouted. But the carriage sped away.

Marco dropped from the tree and landed softly beside her. She felt him take her elbow and help her to her feet, but she was hardly paying attention – she just stared after Filpepi, fury and shock fighting for control over her face.

'Bianca? Are you OK?'

'I don't know,' Bianca said. 'I mean, yes, I'm not hurt. But . . . I don't know what's going on! Filpepi was so kind to us! Why would he have pretended to be something he wasn't just for a few art tips?'

'Well, I don't know about you,' said Marco, 'but I really, *really* think we should stop this wedding.'

Bianca shook herself. 'You're right. Come on. We have to get into the palace – *now*.'

'But how?' Marco asked.

'The mural in Santa Cecilia's, where we came out after the fire!'

Bianca took a deep breath, then they headed out for the Piazza del Kaldi. Marco was right. They could fix this.

The church of Santa Cecilia was empty, but they could hear harmonies echoing through the air. The choir must be practising in one of the back rooms. Bianca crept down the aisle holding her breath, afraid to disturb them and have to explain why they were trying to open a painted door.

She held up the paintbrush and whispered, 'Hidden rooms, secret passages, second city.' The brush's whirring and clicking as it transformed into the key sounded like heavy rattling chains in the quiet of the church.

They quickly let themselves into the secret passage

159

through the heavy oak door in the background of the painting of Santa Cecilia composing her great hymnbook masterpiece. Bianca tried not to look back at the place on the floor where di Lombardi had breathed his last, and shut the door behind them quickly.

'I wonder if di Lombardi had a map,' Marco muttered, as they moved from door to door, peering through windows and keyholes into great houses and chapels all over La Luminosa. 'I think we're getting closer, but it'd be so much easier if we knew which turning to take.'

'Maybe he didn't want it to fall into the wrong hands,' Bianca said, running her fingers over the paintbrush-key. 'Imagine if a thief found his way in here. Or an assassin!' She shuddered at the thought of a stealthy, masked figure climbing silently out of the walls in the middle of the night.

'Bianca, come and look – isn't this in the palace?'

Bianca shook off the vision and went to peer through the little porthole window in a door made entirely of brass. 'Yes! That's the Pearl Courtyard; this must be the cabin door in the fresco of Duke Antonio landing the Pearl at Cittaveccio.'

'We must be just round the corner from the Rose Gallery,' Marco said, putting his head around a turning in the dim passageway. 'So if we want to get to the Duchess's chambers, I think we need to go . . . *this* way.'

He was right. Soon they'd passed the rickety wooden door that looked onto the troupe's dressing room, and then Bianca was peeking through the keyhole into the Duchess's chambers.

It was swarming with maids and serving ladies bustling about, chatting, carrying huge bunches of flowers, cleaning the floor and doing complicated things to big pieces of creamy cloth. Bianca almost didn't notice the Duchess herself – or rather, the imposter – who sat silently on her couch with her hands folded in her lap, her face still creepily impassive. Bianca shuddered, feeling a flare of sympathy for the poor girl, whoever she was.

'No good,' Bianca whispered back to Marco. 'They are preparing for the wedding in there. We'll have to find another way in.'

They passed the Duchess's bedroom – now full of light, and also full of servants – and came to a small, plain, unmarked door. It didn't have a window, and when Bianca knelt to look through the keyhole she couldn't see much except for a large mirror and the corner of a window with muslin drapes drawn across it. The room was dim and silent. Bianca watched for several minutes, and didn't see anyone moving inside.

'I think this one's empty.' She pulled the paintbrush-key from her pocket and carefully, willing it not to make a sound, she turned it in the keyhole. The door swung open. Painted vines brushed the top of her head and she glanced back at the painting. It was an old, crumbling tower, with the magic door half-concealed at its base by the undergrowth.

'Oh, it's a dressing room,' she whispered to Marco, and turned back to the room. Then she caught her breath.

A long rail was suspended from the ceiling beside the

tall mirror. The Duchess's wedding clothes hung on the rail – a white veil, an abundance of petticoats and corseted underthings, and Grand Duchess Angelica's diamond gown, in all its glory. Without any direct light shining on it there was no galaxy of stars reflected around the room, but the multifaceted surface of each diamond still glittered, flashing with every colour of the rainbow.

'It certainly looks the same as the one we saw yesterday in Filpepi's studio,' Marco pointed out. 'Maybe he had the real one, after all.'

'It's so beautiful,' Bianca said, half to herself. 'It's awful – Duchess Catriona should be wearing this on her real wedding day! Instead of some imposter, marrying a villain.'

She reached out a hand, hesitated, put her hand down, and then reached out again. She ought not to touch it. She knew she ought not to. But what could it hurt, really. If it wasn't too fragile to wear to a wedding, it wouldn't be too fragile for her to just touch one of the sleeves . . .

She ran her finger over the surface of a string of diamonds. Or she tried to. Her finger felt something slick move under it, just slightly. The surface didn't feel like gems. It was *sticky*. It was . . .

She stared at the end of her finger, her mouth open.

'It's paint.' She turned it back and forth, watching the white-and-*glimmer* smear glint in the light. 'The dress is covered in . . .' she stopped and peered closer at the dress. She sniffed it, and then knelt down and pinched the lace around the bottom of the dress between her fingers. 'No

162

– it *is*. It is paint!' Marco came to look, and Bianca turned to him, her eyes wide with shock. 'Marco, do you know what this means?'

'Not a clue,' said Marco. 'How could you make a real object out of paint? Outside of a painting?'

'I don't know,' Bianca said softly. 'But apparently I did.'

'*You?*' Marco said. 'How could it be you?'

'I know my work. I painted this lace. I painted half these diamonds . . . and showed Filpepi how to do the rest. But it was inside the painting when I did it!' She stepped back, her hands over her mouth.

'Wow. So Filpepi's painted this right out of the picture!' Marco prodded one of the diamonds with his finger and a sparkling rainbow sheen came off and stuck to him.

'He must have known about the wedding,' Bianca muttered. 'Which means he knew about the imposter, which means . . .'

Marco gasped. 'Bianca! What can change someone's appearance?' He gestured to his own face. '*Make-up*. We use it all the time in our shows. I bet Filpepi painted that girl's face to look just like the Duchess!'

Bianca thought of Rosa and Cosimo and all the other apprentices still working for Filpepi, not knowing his plans for them, and felt sick. 'Master –' she corrected herself. '*Piero* Filpepi has been in on this from the beginning. That's why he threw me out for asking questions: he knew I was getting close to finding out what happened. The Baron and Filpepi are in on this together. I bet he's the one who started the fire, when they thought the poison wasn't going to finish the job,' she added bitterly.

'What can we do?' Marco asked.

'I don't know,' said Bianca fiercely. 'But we have to do something. We have to stop this wedding!'

Chapter Nineteen

'We have about four hours before the wedding,' Bianca said, shutting the door to the dressing room behind her and leaning on the wall of the secret passage. 'What can we do in four hours? How can we prove to everyone that the Duchess isn't herself?'

Marco turned to look at her, and froze. 'Hang on. Move your head.' He grabbed Bianca's shoulders and nudged her aside. 'Look, there's something written here.'

Bianca squinted at the door. He was right – there was something scrawled on the wall next to the door. It was more of that strange half-writing that Marco had found in the back of di Lombardi's notebook. It was painted in a colour almost exactly the same shade as the stone behind it. Bianca thought she could've gone in and out through this door a hundred times and never seen it. She blurred her vision as before, trying to make it coalesce into one word, but before she could make sense of it, Marco made a disappointed noise behind her.

'What, what does it say?' Bianca asked.

'I dunno, it seems like nonsense. *Gold key*. But the key to get in is the same for all these doors, isn't it?'

'I think so.' Bianca turned away from the door. 'I suppose if we need another key later we'll find out. Come on. Maybe if we keep moving one of these doors will take us to the Baron's chambers and we'll be able to find some proof.' She frowned. 'Or maybe we should head back to Filpepi's study and try to sneak in and go through his papers, or something – what do you think?'

She turned back to Marco, but he wasn't there. He was still hanging back by one of the other doors.

'Come on,' she said. Marco waved as if to say yes, but he seemed more interested in stopping to examine the wall every few feet, looking for more of the strange writing. '*Gold key* . . .' he muttered.

Bianca huffed out a breath in frustration. 'Marco, I don't think this is helping!' she snapped.

'No, I can do this!' Marco pointed at the doors to the Duchess's bedroom and the one to her chambers. Look, this one says *gold key* too, and this one says *gold key work*. I think 'gold key' has something to do with the Duchess! And this one – oh.' His face fell as he went cross-eyed looking at the door to the chapel.

Bianca tried to ignore him, but he kept staring at the writing, so she let out a sigh. 'What?'

'*Gold window cross*,' said Marco. 'All right, but I can work this out. I can.'

'No! We shouldn't be wasting time with this!' Bianca

shouted. 'I'm sure Master di Lombardi had a very good reason for labelling these doors, but it's not going to be much help to us or him if we can't avenge his death and stop the Baron stealing the throne!'

Marco shrugged sullenly. 'Fine. Come on, then. Let's try to find a door that will help us.'

Bianca started to run along the passage, but soon turned back with a furious sigh. Marco had gone. She backtracked a few feet and found him at the end of another turning, one that led to a dead end with a single plain wooden door at the end.

'It's just – this one is completely different! It says *sun peril work*.'

'Doesn't sound like a door we should go through, does it?' Bianca said.

'But it's the only one without a colour! Why would this one say *sun*? It could be important! It's better than blindly running into every door!'

'Well, I'm certainly not going into any room labelled "peril", not with only a couple of hours to stop this wedding. And *I've* got the key, so we're going where I say.'

'Stop being so pigheaded, will you? I just think –'

Something registered on the edge of Bianca's hearing and she froze. She held up a hand to stop Marco speaking. Was that an echo she'd heard? It had sounded like a voice – but there couldn't be anyone else in here. Could there? Marco had heard something too – she could see him concentrating, his ears pricking up almost as clearly as if he'd been a cat sensing the approach of a mouse.

'I told you . . .' the faint voice said. 'I told you she should die . . .'

Bianca and Marco stared at each other in horror. *Someone else knew about these passages.*

Bianca gestured for Marco to stay where he was and crept along the passage, hugging the wall, until she came to a corner.

'She should be dead by now,' said a voice, frighteningly clear. Bianca felt all the blood draining from her face. It was Filpepi.

'It would've been neater if you'd killed her before the first ball,' replied the Baron da Russo.

'Don't you think I tried that?' snarled Filpepi. 'I couldn't find her!'

Marco snuck up alongside her and grabbed her sleeve. She nodded and they both tiptoed as quickly as they could back along the passage and around the next corner. Marco skidded to a halt, peering carefully around the corner of the passage, waiting. Bianca shifted from foot to foot, twisting the paintbrush-key between her fingers, listening to the voices. What on earth would they do if they caught her and Marco here?

'The old fool must have hidden her here somewhere,' said Filpepi. Bianca clenched her fists. How *dare* he talk about her master like that! 'If only I'd found his notebooks. There must be a clue. We'll find her and finish the job.'

'But how long will that take?' asked the Baron.

'As long as she stays hidden until after the wedding. Then –'

'No, that's not good enough,' said the Baron, sharply. 'We need to eliminate her, *now*, or all of this could be for nothing. Do you want that?'

'We'll find her,' Filpepi grumbled. 'Don't worry.'

Marco suddenly pulled back from the corner, so sharply the back of his head nearly collided with Bianca's nose. He made a desperate face and pointed to the passage. Bianca knew exactly what he meant.

They're coming this way.

She turned, looking to see where this part of the passage led, and her heart sank. It was the dead end, and the door marked *peril*.

Of course it is.

Marco glared at her pointedly and mouthed, *They're going to kill us!*

Bianca nodded and ran to the door, the key ready in her hand. If she was going to be facing peril anyway . . .

Marco sidled back to the corner to sneak another look. Bianca turned to glance at him and he made a frantic winding motion with his hand. Bianca fumbled the key into the lock and turned it as softly as she could.

There was a small *click*, just as Filpepi said, 'Soon, my Lord Baron. All the passages will be opened, and the two cities will be one.'

What did that mean? Bianca was frowning as she threw open the door, bundled Marco past her, leapt inside and silently shut it behind them.

She leaned on the door, her forehead pressed to the cool wood, waiting for her heartbeat to slow down. Had they

169

been seen? If Filpepi and the Baron could get inside the passages, could they get through the door too?

'Bianca . . .' said Marco. 'Look.'

Bianca turned, and gasped.

It was a studio – or a workshop – no, it was both. But it was like the ideal of those rooms, the kind of studio that Bianca built in her dreams. Warm light filtered down from the windows in the high, vaulted ceiling. Gleaming tools lined the walls, neat piles of sketches and notes sat beside workstations for blowing glass, working copper and brass and iron, stitching huge leather canvases and carving wood. Rows of easels, large enough to hold canvases the size of small rooms, some empty and some with canvases under white sheets, and a cabinet with a glass front and a hefty lock that held *hundreds* of ingredient pots . . .

And then there were the contraptions.

Bianca stepped into the room and put an entranced hand out to touch the copper nose of a Vehicle for Traversing Underneath the Canal Surface. It was a small, bullet-shaped steamcart, just like the picture in di Lombardi's notebooks. Tears sprang to her eyes as she glanced up and caught sight of a Machine to Amplify the Sound of a Violin and an artificial arm with a perfectly carved, articulated hand.

'You said he never built any of these things,' Marco said, in a voice thick with awe.

'He never showed us,' Bianca muttered. She picked up the artificial arm and flexed its elbow gently. 'We all knew he *dreamed* about these things, but, but he . . . he never

170

told us he'd *made* them!' She wiped her eyes on her sleeve. 'Why wouldn't he – oh, this is amazing! Look at this!' she grabbed Marco's hand, dragged him past the underwater steamcart and pointed at the contraption behind it, a sleek cabin of polished wood, a little like a boat and a little like a steamcart, with glass tubes running across its surface like veins and long leather wings, like a bat's, folded neatly to its sides. '*Necessary Parts for a Flying Machine,*' she said. 'Except it's not in parts any more.'

'Are you all right?' Marco asked.

Bianca nodded. 'It's just that . . . it's all so amazing . . .' she said, beginning to grin. 'I never realized . . .'

Marco gave her a slightly frightened look, but then smiled. 'Well, good. We can hide out here till the Baron and Filpepi have gone, and then we can go and help the Duchess.'

'No, I think you were right,' Bianca admitted. 'This place is important. Filpepi wanted to find my master's notebooks, didn't he?' She gestured around at the piles of sketches and books on each of the workstations. 'I bet what he's searching for is in here somewhere. Let's look!'

Marco ran to the end of the row of easels, while Bianca moved methodically between the different crafts, flipping through designs for pictures and statues and machines, searching for anything to do with the Duchess or the Baron or Filpepi or the Grand Duchess's dress. Nothing particularly caught her eye – except for the fact that a lot of the instructions were so technical she could barely understand them. She bit her lip as she searched, terrified that she'd miss something.

171

'Bianca? Come and have a look at this!'

Marco was waving a large sketchbook in the air. She sprinted over to him, vaulting over part of the underwater steamcart in her hurry.

'It looks like the sketches for the Duchess's Ascension painting,' Marco said, as Bianca peered at it. 'Except it's not the same at all. It's a portrait!'

The sketch was in di Lombardi's favourite blue chalk. It was a portrait of Duchess Catriona. She was sitting on a low couch, laughing. Wide windows behind her showed a view from high up, out over the city. The sketch wasn't enchanted, but even so, Bianca felt her heart tighten at the sheer skill; the curtains looked like they were stirring in a soft breeze, the light came in through the windows, and the Duchess's face wore a look of sweet, intelligent contentment.

'Yes, that's definitely the White Tower, just like the painting for the Ascension.' Bianca frowned. 'But that painting didn't have the Duchess in it. Yet in this sketch . . . Here she is . . .'

And then, suddenly, Bianca gasped and looked down at the sketches again, examining the background, checking every detail against her memory.

'What?' said Marco. 'What have you seen?'

'It's not what I've seen – it's what Master di Lombardi *didn't* see!' Bianca cried out. 'Don't you get it?'

Marco gave her a blank look. 'No.'

'Think about it, Marco!' Bianca was almost hopping from foot to foot with excitement now. 'Don't you see

172

what this means? What were we saying before? We thought there was something wrong with the painting, there was something in it he didn't expect. What if there was something . . . *missing*?'

'You mean – he painted the Duchess, but when he unveiled the picture, she'd been painted over?'

'No,' said Bianca. 'I mean when he unveiled the picture . . . she had *gone*.'

Chapter Twenty

'You are mad,' Marco said flatly.

Bianca shook her head vigorously. 'I can paint things and make them real,' she said. 'I can make space and light and things that feel like metal when they're just paint – and think about the dress!'

'But not life,' Marco exclaimed.

'No. An illusion of life,' Bianca said. 'I've never seen it done like *this*,' she admitted. 'Usually they just breathe and smile and repeat simple patterns. Plus, Master di Lombardi obviously didn't mean for this to happen.'

A gleam lit up Marco's eyes. 'What if Master di Lombardi did all the work, made her lifelike enough to move and speak, and Filpepi lifted her out of her painting, just like he did with the dress?'

'It's more possible than a secret identical twin, right? And we haven't found evidence of any magic accomplice who could have disguised someone as the Duchess.' Bianca blew out a long breath. 'Filpepi would've had access to the painting once it was moved into the palace. Plus,' she looked down at the smiling Duchess in the blue chalk sketch. 'Duchess Catriona was always painted without her birthmark, but she didn't cover it in real life. The new Duchess doesn't have it. If Filpepi was creating an imposter's face from scratch he would've included it.'

Marco nodded. 'Well, this is completely mad. But you have to be right.'

Bianca dragged her hands through her hair. 'The Baron should've killed the Duchess before the first ball . . .' she suppressed a shudder. 'But he didn't, and Master di Lombardi hid her somewhere. That means she's still alive! All we have to do is find her and we can prove the other one is an imposter.'

'Let's keep searching these tunnels.' Marco closed the sketchbook and put it back on the easel where he'd found it. 'But we need to wait here until the Baron and Filpepi have gone.'

'Agreed.' Bianca looked around at the wonderful crafts and mechanisms. 'Maybe there's something in here we can use against the Baron?'

Bianca walked between the machines and inventions, occasionally pushing switches or tapping dials, hoping for inspiration. She reached up and wound the tiny lever behind the head of a beautiful model of a bluebird made of silver and brass. There was a sound of a mainspring creaking and clockwork whirring, and Bianca gasped and jumped back as the bird seemed to spring into life. It tilted its head and looked at her, snapped its beak twice with a tiny *clickclick* sound, and then leapt into the air and fluttered, whirring around her head and up into the sunlight, its metal wings slicing the air. She watched as it approached the high windows and batted at them.

Bianca frowned. She wished she could open the windows, but they were so high up . . .

Then a glint of copper in the sunlight caught her eye. It was a thick cord that ran down from the windows to a handle on the other side of the room. She ran over and turned the handle, and looked up. The windows slid away smoothly, without so much as a creak, and the bird whistled and chirped and vanished into the open sky.

'I wonder if those windows go somewhere in the real world,' she muttered. 'Is that the real sky? Or another kind of doorway?'

Not all of the inventions worked as well as the little bird. Bianca found a similar metal mouse and wound it up, but it only went *putputput* and then one of its ears fell off with a sad little *sproing*.

'Well, if we can't use any of this stuff as a weapon, how about a distraction?' Marco suggested, picking up the fallen brass ear. 'Maybe we can disrupt the wedding and give ourselves more time.'

'But how could we . . .' Bianca began, looking around the room. She trailed off as her gaze caught and held on the gleaming glass, copper, polished wood and neatly folded leather of di Lombardi's flying machine. She looked from the small cabin to the bright blue overhead and back again. 'If we could fly out of here . . .'

'That's a very big "if",' Marco said.

Bianca examined the pile of sketches and measurements and calculations on the glassblowing bench nearest the flying machine. 'It has to be worth a try. It looks like maybe it could work – it needs some kind of fuel for the steam pumps, um . . .' she cast around. 'Try that locker over there.'

Marco gave a half salute and ran over to a large cabinet with iron doors and a large bolt on the outside. 'Gas bottles!' he called back across the room. 'Will that do?'

Bianca looked at the mechanics of the machine. There was no coal burner, but there was a kind of hot air balloon. It seemed to run hot steam down iron tubes and into the wings. 'Gas might be just the thing,' she told him.

Marco carried over two thick glass bottles with airtight stoppers and put them down beside the cabin of the flying machine. 'Well, let's hope you're right, because I don't fancy being inside this thing if you're wrong. We'll suffocate first, and then explode.'

'I'm almost certainly not wrong. Probably.' Bianca pulled open the door to the cabin and leaned inside. It had two seats, side by side, open to the air on top like the seats on the front of a horse cart. Except that instead of reins and horses in front of the seats, there were levers and buttons and an enormous winch and a big glass screen. Behind the seats there was the steam-burner-thing – Bianca thought she could see where the gas would go – and pipes that ran across the cabin and underneath the wings.

'Water,' she muttered. 'For steam, we'll need water.

There's a container here that slides out.' She pulled on a wide copper bucket and it slid out smoothly and clanged onto the floor. 'I think it'll need both of us to lift it.'

Marco grabbed one side of the bucket and Bianca picked up the other, and together they heaved it across the room.

'Where's the tap? *Is* there a tap?' asked Bianca.

'I think I saw one over by the easels.'

They picked their way carefully past fragile confections of cogs and glass and wheels, over to the row of easels. Bianca saw a sink beside the cabinet of paint ingredients and turned towards it, but something snagged her ankle and she tripped. She reached out to try to catch herself, but her hand just closed on a fistful of white cloth. She landed on the ground, and gasped as the sheet, the bucket and Marco all fell on top of her.

'Oof!' she groaned. 'Get off!'

But Marco didn't reply, or move. He just sat there with his elbow digging into her stomach.

'Oi!' She sat up and opened her mouth to snap at Marco, but then her gaze fell on the thing he was staring at.

It was another painting of the Duchess, almost lifesize, seated on a plain wooden chair. It had been under the sheet that she'd just dragged off the easel. This picture obviously wasn't alive – actually, she seemed almost flat, as if di Lombardi hadn't bothered to add any magic to the figure at all. It wasn't the figure that was extraordinary – it was the fact that on the right side of the painting there was a doorknob and a keyhole hanging in space, without a door to belong to. They certainly looked real. The

178

sunshine from the high windows gleamed off the brass doorknob.

Bianca struggled to her feet and helped Marco disentangle his feet from the white sheet.

'Where d'you think it goes?' Marco said, peering down to look through the keyhole. 'It's too dark; I can't see anything.'

Bianca rolled the paintbrush-key between her fingers for a moment, then took the painting down from the easel and set it carefully against a bare patch of wall.

'Only one way to find out.' She reached into the painting, closing her hand over the gleaming doorknob. Her heart pattered in her chest, like the tiny wings of the mechanical bird beating against her ribcage, as she slipped the key into the lock. It went in smoothly and turned with a barely-audible metal sound. Bianca pushed on the doorknob and the whole painting seemed to swing inwards, as if it was opening a passage in the wall.

Inside, Bianca and Marco found themselves looking at a small sitting room with a comfortably stuffed couch, a roaring fire, a bookshelf, and a low table. A handful of sketches in charcoal were scattered over the table and there was a book propped open on the couch. A large, unmade bed sat in one corner.

She walked hesitantly into the room, her heart in her throat.

'Um. Hello? Is . . . Is anyone here?'

'Finally!' said a familiar voice. Bianca spun around. Duchess Catriona – the *real* Duchess Catriona – was sitting

179

on a chair in the corner of the room. She jumped up, folded her arms and gazed expectantly at them. 'Bianca, hello! Is di Lombardi finally ready for me? It's been *days*! I'm almost out of food. What is going on out there?'

Bianca gulped. How could she even begin to explain what had happened while the Duchess had been safely locked away?

Chapter Twenty-one

'He said he'd fetch me himself, but it's been so long I was starting to worry! Oh, and Marco! Has Master di Lombardi sent you to entertain me? I've been *so* bored cooped up here by myself for three days, and without so much as a single birthday present. I thought . . . What?'

Bianca stared at the Duchess, catching her breath before she could bring herself to answer. She was so much like the imposter – except messier, more imperfect, and bursting with life and energy. Her birthmark wrinkled on her cheek as she smiled at them. Her red hair was loose to her waist, much longer than Bianca had ever realised, and her velvet skirt was on slightly askew. Bianca guessed she wasn't used to dressing without her maid.

Now the Duchess was frowning. Bianca swept a hurried curtsey.

'Bianca, stop bobbing and answer me,' Duchess Catriona said, worry vibrating in her voice. 'Is everything all right? Was the Baron apprehended?'

'Um . . . no,' said Marco. He kept glancing from Bianca to the Duchess. Bianca guessed it was up to her to explain what was happening. But she couldn't get the words out.

'Well! What's the use of any of you?' Duchess Catriona threw up her hands. 'Honestly, tell your master I don't care if he is the greatest spymaster I could wish for, I won't stay another day in this gloomy little place if he doesn't come and paint me some *daylight*, right away!' The Duchess was joking, throwing away her words with a smile and a wave of her arm, but the smile was brittle and tense.

Bianca swallowed. 'Your Highness, I am so sorry. Master di Lombardi is dead.'

The brittle smile vanished altogether, and Duchess Catriona caught her breath. 'No . . . he can't be . . .' she took a few steps into the room and sank down on the couch, clutching at her skirts. 'How? Come here at once and tell me everything.'

Bianca and Marco walked into the room and sank to their knees in front of the Duchess's couch.

'We think – well, we're pretty certain – that the Baron and Filpepi killed him,' Bianca said. 'He was poisoned with arsenic in his wine, and then while he was recovering, his house was burned down and he died from the smoke.'

Duchess Catriona sniffed and swiped at her eyes with her sleeve. Bianca reached into a pocket and pulled out a handkerchief – the same one, embroidered with the sun emblem of La Luminosa, that the Duchess had given her three days ago. The Duchess looked at it and her eyes welled up even more, but she smiled gratefully at Bianca.

'Go on,' she said, her voice steady through her tears. 'Piero Filpepi, you say? I didn't know he was involved. I suppose he would have a reason to want Master di Lombardi out of the way.'

'If we may, Your Highness,' Marco said, 'what do you know about the Baron? What did Master di Lombardi know?'

'He was sure the Baron was planning to assassinate me,' the Duchess said. 'After so many years ruling the city as Regent, he just couldn't let go of all that power, so he planned to have me killed. I have no heir and no other family – he would be the only one with a claim to the throne. Master di Lombardi hid me in this painted room until the day of the coronation, so that I would be safe until I could take the throne. But now, tell me,' she clenched the handkerchief tight in one fist. 'What moves has the Baron made since I disappeared? What does he think has happened to me? What has he told people about my disappearance?'

'Um . . . well, it's a bit . . .' Bianca glanced at Marco, who shrugged. 'Filpepi used Master di Lombardi's painting of you, and some magic of his own, to . . . to turn the painting into a living creature. Sort of living, anyway. As far as the people are concerned, you're not missing – you're still living in the palace. They made a fake Duchess. And put her in your place.'

Duchess Catriona stared at Bianca, her eyes narrowing in confusion and then in anger as this sunk in. 'A forgery!'

'Though she's not behaving at all like you,' Marco added.

'She's just a puppet for the Baron and Filpepi to control. And she's, um . . .'

'She's marrying the Baron,' said Bianca quickly, hoping if she said it quickly it would be easier, like peeling fixing glue off her arm. 'And the marriage will take place in the next few hours.'

Duchess Catriona seized up her skirts and ran for the door out of the painting.

'Your Highness!' Marco called after her as he and Bianca got to their feet and ran after her. 'Wait! We have to have a plan, you can't just –'

'I can *just* whatever I like,' Duchess Catriona called back over her shoulder as she raced through the room. '*I* am the ruler of this city! And I shall make sure that my traitorous Baron never, ever forgets it!'

She wrenched open the door to the secret passages and slipped through in a rustle of wonky red velvet skirts. Bianca gave Marco a despairing glance and hurried after her.

In the dim, flickering light of the passage, they saw the Duchess reach the dead end turn and hesitate, looking left and right. Bianca caught up with her just as she sprang into a run, the wrong way.

'No, Your Highness,' Bianca gasped. 'We should go to the chapel. This way!'

Duchess Catriona paused and looked back, suspiciously.

'We need you,' Bianca said. 'We need you to show them the imposter is a fake. We can get in through the Santa Juanita fresco in the chapel.'

184

'Let's go then!' said the Duchess, clearly still fuming.

'But please, slow down a little, just for a . . .' It was no good. The Duchess swept back past Bianca and down the passage. Marco almost tripped as he turned the corner at a run and Bianca's heart raced as her feet pounded the corridor trying to keep up. The Duchess came to a halt outside the chapel door and rattled the handle, but it was locked. Bianca had the key out in her hand even as she got to the door, but she hesitated, looking up at the Duchess one more time.

'Please, let's –'

'Bianca, I am your Duchess. I command you to open this door!'

Bianca exchanged one last apprehensive look with Marco, and then bobbed a curtsey. 'Yes, Your Highness.' She turned the key in the lock.

Duchess Catriona threw open the door and strode through with her head high, Bianca and Marco trailing in her wake.

The chapel was full of people. Lords and ladies in jewel-coloured coats and gowns thronged the pews. More priests than Bianca had ever seen before were standing in an ordered huddle around the altar, dressed in their best white and gold embroidered robes and skullcaps. Bianca gulped as she noticed that the walls of the chapel were lined with what looked like almost the entire palace guard, their gold-polished armour gleaming around the room like a sparkling metal ribbon. Filpepi was there too, standing by the Captain of the Guard, gazing down the aisle with pride.

At the end of the aisle, the fake Duchess and the Baron da Russo stood with their hands clasped, ready to take their vows. She was wearing the false diamond dress. The sunlight streamed through the stained glass window behind the altar and hit the painted diamonds, sending a thousand rainbow sparkles flying from it whenever she moved.

Slowly, like a ripple passing across a still pond, everyone in the chapel turned and gasped at the sight of the real Duchess Catriona, her hair loose and her dress unkempt, flanked by an artist's apprentice and a boy tumbler.

'Stop! Stop this at once! By command of the Duchess!' she shouted. 'Guards, arrest this man and his imposter bride!'

'How dare you?' The Baron dropped the imposter's hands and turned to gape at the Duchess, as if this was the strangest thing he'd ever seen. He wasn't a bad actor – although, Bianca guessed, some of that shock was real. She smirked and folded her arms.

'How dare . . .' the Duchess clenched her fists and growled in frustration. 'How dare *I*? I am your Duchess!'

'Bianca!' Filpepi stepped forward. 'Is this some kind of revenge? Against me? Against our fair Duchess?'

'No, Filpepi, *this* is the real Duchess!' Bianca yelled, swelling with anger and pride that she could stand up to Filpepi at last. '*You* created that imposter to take her place!'

'Baron, Duchess, my Lords and Ladies,' Filpepi advanced down the aisle. 'Please do not judge this girl too harshly. Only this morning I had to dismiss her from her position for upsetting Duchess Catriona. This is obviously some kind of prank. It is in *very bad taste*, Bianca.'

'You had me fooled, Filpepi,' said Bianca. 'But no more.'

'Bianca,' he said, looking into her eyes, 'perhaps I was too harsh on you. You are a talented painter – the most talented of all my apprentices. Perhaps if you calm down I will reconsider my dismissal of you. Perhaps even accelerate your learning and set you up with your own studio. You could employ your own apprentices . . .'

Bianca scowled at him, but her skin was starting to crawl. She knew he was trying to bribe her, offering her everything she'd ever wanted. But it wasn't enough. She shook her head in disgust.

Some of the lords and ladies were whispering to each other, staring at her and pointing. And she couldn't help noticing that none of the guards had moved . . .

'Filpepi, you are under arrest,' Duchess Catriona hissed through her clenched teeth. 'Guards, seize both these men *right now* . . .'

'Who is this common wench you two have dressed up like Duchess Catriona?' said the Baron. 'I admit the likeness is quite good, but how could you think she could compare to the sweet jewel of our city?' He gestured back to the imposter Duchess, whose face remained completely blank, as if it were the wedding in a story book being disrupted, and not her own.

'How could you think that's her?' Marco spoke up. 'Look at her, really look! You're all blinded by the dress and the pretty hair – she doesn't even care that someone's come to take her throne!'

Bianca gave him a grateful smile, but if the assembled

nobles were beginning to come around to their point of view, it all came to an end when Filpepi leaned in to Duchess Catriona, with a cruel smile.

'Whoever you are, wench,' he said, 'you should go back to the gutter where you came from.'

Duchess Catriona lashed out with one foot and kicked Filpepi hard in the shins.

'Common wench?' she yelled. '*Sweet jewel*? I am your Duchess! How *dare* you patronise me in such a manner! *This* is for Master di Lombardi –' she kicked him again, '– And *this* is for presuming to replace me with a painted doll!' And again. 'Besides, I am far prettier that that fake!'

'Guards, seize her!' roared the Baron. He pointed at Duchess Catriona, and as he did, Bianca could see that the palm and fingers of his hand glittered. The paint was still wet on the imposter's gown. He was going to need to scrub for hours with paint remover to get that off.

'Look! Look at his hand!' Bianca yelled, but the roar of nobles making up their minds and spurring on the guards to seize the Duchess drowned it out. The guards may not have known who to believe at first, but now their instincts told them to advance on the Duchess, lowering their spears.

Duchess Catriona let out a roar of frustration and threw herself past Filpepi, down the aisle and ran at the imposter. The Baron managed to sweep her out of the way just in time and the Duchess caught herself on the altar.

The imposter seemed to wake up a little – if nothing else, she looked into the Duchess's furious eyes and some

188

kind of self-preservation kicked in. She gave a little wet yelping sound and bolted, out through the nave door and up the spiral stairs that led up to the Duchess's roof-garden. The real Duchess was on her heels before anyone could stop her, scattering priests and hesitant guards as she elbowed past them.

Marco tried to follow them, but Filpepi tripped him and he narrowly avoided a spiking from a guard's spear. Bianca grabbed him by the shirt just in time to pull him back. 'Not that way! Come on!'

She leapt back into the painting and bundled Marco through the door, slammed it shut and locked it firmly behind them.

Chapter Twenty-two

'What're you doing?' Marco gasped. 'We've got to follow them!'

'Do you want to get yourself impaled? I don't think we're going to get through that way.'

He looked around desperately. 'There's got to be somewhere else we can get through. Or they'll catch the Duchess, and the Baron and his painted wife will have the throne!'

His painted wife.

His painted . . .

'She's made of paint!'

'I know! That's what I said! We've got to –'

'No, you don't get it!' Bianca gripped Marco's shoulders and squeezed them hard. 'She's made out of paint, and he's got paint on his hands, and there's only one way – Marco, you're a *genius*.'

She turned and pounded down the passage. Behind her, she heard Marco's feet break into a run, but she didn't look back. She didn't have time. She hit the door to di

Lombardi's secret workshop key-first and barely paused as she turned the lock and threw it open.

'Get the water in the bucket,' she yelled to Marco. 'We're going to use the flying machine!'

'If you say so,' said Marco. He didn't sound convinced, but he ran to the big copper bucket and lifted it to the sink and started to fill it with water.

Bianca jumped into the front seat of the flying machine and loaded the two bottles of gas into their places in the back of the wooden cabin, beneath the burner. Then she jumped out the other side and ran for the cabinet full of paint ingredients.

'Come on, come on, you must be . . . you must have . . . ah!' She opened a plain wooden door at the bottom of the cabinet and tugged out an enormous can of paint remover, bigger than her head, with a handle and a lid. She grabbed a palette knife and levered it open. A cloud of ether and orange essence hit her and she recoiled, her eyes watering, and put the lid back on quickly.

'So what are we going to do?' Marco groaned, heaving the bucket full of water carefully across the room to the machine. 'Crash it into the chapel roof?'

'No!' Bianca lugged the can into the cabin of the flying machine, grabbed the notebook full of instructions and calculations, and threw them in too. 'This is Master di Lombardi's patented paint remover. It's got to be ten times as strong as Filpepi's. This stuff can strip *anything*.' She helped Marco lift the bucket of water into place on top of the boiler and then pressed down on the lever that opened the gas bottle and struck two pieces of flint together. A flame sprang up and licked around the bottom of the copper bucket. Bianca slid shut the hatch between the flame and the cabin and sat down in the driver's seat.

'Right,' said Marco. 'Now we just need to get to her.' Bianca saw him looking apprehensively up at the blue sky beyond the open hatch, and then down at the heavy wood, metal and glass contraption they were sitting in.

'It'll work. I'm sure it will,' Bianca lied. 'Turn that handle as fast as you can.'

Marco grabbed the long handle she'd pointed to and spun it until it was a blur. With a creaking sound, the leather wings folded out to their full length. Bianca watched the dial in front of her, marked *steam pressure*, flicker upwards as the water in the bucket started to heat.

'On my mark,' she said, 'pull out both the stops in front of you, and then . . .'

'Then *what*?' Marco asked.

'. . . hang on,' she told him. 'And pray.'

The steam was starting to build, pouring through the glass tubes all along the edges of the cabin. Bianca felt hidden mechanisms underneath them start to whirr and judder. The whole cabin shook. The needle on the steam pressure dial crept slowly, slowly up.

'Now!' Bianca yelled over the sound of creaking wood and metal.

Marco yanked the stops out of their places. There was a hiss and a pulsating sound like a rubber bag inflating and deflating, and the flying machine began to move. The wings beat up and down and it bobbed on a cushion of air for a moment. Marco and Bianca both yelped and grabbed onto the sides of the cabin, then Bianca made herself take hold of the two levers in front of her. She glanced at the notebook one more time, and turned both levers down. The wings responded, flapping faster, sending more and more steam through the ducts, and the flying machine rose into the air with a *putt-putt-putt-whirr-putt-whirr* sound.

'It's working!' Marco yelled.

'I have to steer us through the roof,' Bianca shouted back. 'Tell me if we're going to hit anything!'

'Not so far.' Marco twisted in his seat to get a better look. 'Keep going . . . that's it . . . I can't believe we're flying!' He peered over the side, down at the huge workshop, as the wings on the machine flapped harder and harder.

'Eyes on the sky!' Bianca cried.

'Oh right. You're fine – now just a bit forwards . . .' Bianca let the levers snap back to parallel and pressed down on a pedal at her feet. The flying machine lurched alarmingly, tipping forwards. 'That's enough, that's enough!' Marco said as they came level. 'Now up. Up!'

Bianca put all her weight down on the levers, and in a few seconds they had risen through the roof and out into the sunshine.

'Wow!' Bianca gasped as they left the workshop behind. 'We are in the real world, after all!'

The city of La Luminosa was laid out beneath them,

the canals glinting merrily, criss-crossed with tall shadows of buildings in the late afternoon sunlight. No one but the birds had ever seen it from this height. The flying machine soared up and Bianca steered it around in a wide circle, ignoring Marco's yelping as they banked to the left and he clung onto the sides of the cabin.

Di Lombardi's secret workshop was right by the city walls, hidden away behind a stand of tall cypress trees. Bianca steered the flying machine around it once, and then levelled it and put her foot down. Water bubbled and steam hissed and the wings flapped like a bat fluttering around a night-lamp, and they cut through the air towards the palace.

From high above it was stunning. It stood at the centre of the city, a strange puzzle of courtyards and gardens and long sun-baked halls, with the White Tower high above, reflecting the sun into Bianca's eyes. The wind whipped her hair around her face as the flying machine juddered and swooped.

'There!' Marco cried. 'I can see them – they're still fighting!'

Bianca banked the flying machine and peered out. Not that far below, she could see the Duchess's roof-garden with its rows of beautiful blooming trees and flowers. In its centre, a figure in a dress that sparkled and glinted so brightly that it was difficult to look at was locked in battle with another whose red hair flew around her shoulders. All around them, guards stood with their spears half-lifted, as if unsure what to do. The Baron and Filpepi were screaming at the Captain of the Guard, but he was shaking his head and yelling back. Confused nobles stood all around. They'd been watching the two Duchesses, but now they were mostly pointing up at the flying machine, shouting their disbelief.

'Here, swap seats with me. Just keep these levers straight. And try to hold us steady!' Bianca climbed over Marco, grabbed the can of paint remover and tore off the lid.

'Don't miss!' he yelled.

'Thanks,' Bianca said. She leaned over the side of the cabin, trying to lock her knees into the wood against the lurching of the machine. 'Here goes . . .'

She held her breath, aimed as best she could, and tipped the mixture right on top of the fighting Duchesses. It splashed down on them both, coating them in steaming, stinking mixture. Duchess Catriona's hands slipped off the imposter, slick with melted paint. The imposter recoiled, flailing her sparkling arms, trying to shake off the mixture, but it was no use. Splatters of paint hit the flowers and trees and the shiny breastplates of the guards.

The painted girl began to come apart. Bianca saw her hand fall off the end of her arm, splash on the ground and form into puddles. Her knees melted and she fell down. Her red hair ran down her back like a river, and one of her eyes began to slide down her cheek. She collapsed in a heap, and a few seconds later it was all over – all that was left of her was a spreading, glimmering pool of brownish-white goo at the real Duchess's feet.

Duchess Catriona wiped herself down, spreading paint

and remover over her dress. 'Bianca! Couldn't your aim be a little surer?' she said, shooting a furious glance up at the flying machine.

The guards scurried to gather around their Duchess as she turned on the Baron and Filpepi.

'And now, Captain, *if you don't mind*,' she yelled, 'seize those traitors!'

The Captain of the Guard pulled out his sword and his men drew in, circling the two villains. Bianca grinned in triumph. They had nowhere to go now! The Baron was panicking, his red face even redder and more swollen than usual, and Filpepi dropped to his knees.

But he wasn't surrendering. Bianca squinted. He was pulling a piece of charcoal from his pocket, dragging it over the ground in front of him . . .

'Be careful!' she yelled down to the guards.

Filpepi's drawing suddenly took on a strange gleaming texture, and Bianca gasped as she realised that he'd drawn a lifelike handle on one of the large paving stones on the garden path. He reached down and tugged on it and the stone came up in his hand.

A trapdoor! 'They're going to escape!' she shouted, though she didn't think they could hear her – everyone on the roof was shouting too, and diving to grab hold of the Baron and Filpepi. But it was no good. Filpepi pushed the Baron through the trapdoor and jumped through himself.

Bianca's breath caught in her chest as she gazed down through the hole. Just before the stone slammed back, she thought she could see the pointed spires of dark towers.

Blood-red flags fluttering in an impossible wind. Black rooftops sending out white smoke. A black river, like a canal at night but without any of the stars reflected in its depths. Buildings of black stone and street lamps that glittered like the diamonds but shed almost no light. It was as if she'd looked down into the ground and seen a glimpse of a strange, dark city, streaked with vivid colour.

Then the stone slammed back into the ground. The Captain of the Guard tried to pull it up again, but the handle was just a scribbled drawing. Duchess Catriona stamped her foot and let out a scream of rage.

'Did you see that?' Bianca muttered.

'They escaped! Where did they go?' Marco said. 'Back to the passages? I couldn't see down there, it was too dark.'

'I don't think so . . .' Bianca said. She sat back in her seat as Marco started to steer the flying machine downwards, towards one of the big courtyards in the palace grounds, fiddling with the buttons that would release a blast of steam to cushion their landing. But she wasn't thinking about landing – or even about crashing.

She thought she knew where the Baron and Filpepi had gone.

Hidden rooms, secret passages . . .
Second city.

Epilogue

The dark streets are cool under my feet. The water in the canal is still and silent, like a silky black ribbon winding around the buildings. I look up and there are no stars and no moon in the sky. Light spills out of the buildings, instead of in pouring into them – flickering candlelight and bright blue crackling thunder-lamps.

Strange, pale people pass me on the street without giving me a second glance. Most of them wear black, or greys and browns so dark they are almost black. Every so often someone passes me who looks different – their clothes are of finer, deeper opaque shades, and streaked with bright, bright colours. A lady with a scarf in vivid green stops to look down into the canal. Her reflection is almost invisible except for the flash of colour around her throat.

I walk into a square, between high, looming buildings, and blink in the sudden glare. A bed of glowing golden flowers wavers in a breeze I can't feel on my skin.

*I want to stay and pick the flowers, but I can't. Something's
calling me. Dragging me away. I try to fight it.*

I want to stay.

This place feels like . . .

home.

'Bianca! It's about to start!'

Bianca woke with a splutter and blinked, almost
blinded by the bright sunlight. Rosa was shaking her
shoulder.

'Don't drop off now,' Rosa said, smiling affectionately.
'You've had such an ordeal, you deserve to see this!'

Bianca tried to shake off the dream with a toss of her
head, and sat up straighter on her chair. She looked around
at the rows and rows of chairs that had been set out in
the Grand Courtyard. Every one of them was occupied.
There were lords and ladies in their finery, priests, nobles,
and other people too – representatives from every profes-
sion in La Luminosa. Everyone had sent an envoy, from
the masters of commerce to the people who dredged the
canals in the winter. Bianca smiled. The message was clear:
Duchess Catriona wanted the world to know that she was
going to be Duchess of the *whole* city.

Including the new Royal-Artist-In-Residence, Bianca
thought, with pride that bubbled up from her very core.
She looked down at the chunky gold ring with the sun
emblem engraved on its surface. She would take her new
post very seriously.

She spotted Marco, sitting with his father and the rest

200

of the troupe, and sent him a bright smile. He waved back, making the bells and ribbons on his costume jingle.

The apprentices had been given the finest seats in the house, almost at the front of the audience. They weren't quite as well-dressed as the nobles around them, but they'd been up since dawn scrubbing and preparing, and they were each probably cleaner than they'd ever been in their lives.

Bianca had been walking the streets of the dark city all night in her dreams. She must have been deeply asleep, because the dreams were so vivid – but when she woke up she didn't feel like she'd had a minute's rest. She didn't know how she could get just a single glimpse of a place and then build the whole thing in her mind. The dark city felt so real, it was as if she was remembering it, rather than imagining it. Was this the second city that the Baron and Filpepi had wanted to join with La Luminosa?

A blast of trumpets rang out over the crowd, and Bianca rubbed the sleep from her eyes and sat up straight. Children with fluttering rainbow-coloured ribbons on the end of poles processed down the aisle between the seats and into the courtyard, surrounding the podium where the golden throne of La Luminosa stood.

Bianca shifted uncomfortably at the thought that those men were still out there, somewhere, and that nobody from La Luminosa could find them. The Duchess had sworn that her guards would never give up the search, but she'd also insisted that her coronation go ahead as soon as possible. Bianca couldn't blame her.

Then there was another fanfare, and everyone in the crowd swivelled in their chairs to get the first look at their new ruler.

Duchess Catriona stepped out into the blazing sunshine, following slowly after the children with their ribbons, holding the sun-sceptre in her hands. The crowd caught their breath at the beauty of her. Her dress was a deep, royal purple and trimmed with spun gold that sparkled in the light. Her hair was plaited and woven with silver thread. She reached the platform, took her place on the throne, and the Archbishop placed the heavy gold-and-ruby crown on her head and a golden orb in her other hand.

She looked so perfect, Bianca's heart gave an uneasy thud. What if this was all too good to be true? What if this wasn't really her Duchess?

Then the newly crowned ruler of La Luminosa caught Bianca's eye, looked down at the purple of her skirt, and just for the tiniest fraction of a second, she stuck out her tongue.

Bianca gave a snort of laughter. Cosimo elbowed her and gave her a fierce look, which didn't help at all.

The crowd rose to hail their Duchess, and Bianca applauded along with the rest. She glanced up at the blue sky, and imagined di Lombardi soaring overhead, keeping pace with the angels in his marvellous flying machine. She just wished he could have been here to see it all. Tears came into Bianca's eyes at the thought of her master. Maybe he would have been able to explain the truth behind the 'second city' he'd tried to tell her about with his dying words.

The image of herself walking the streets of the dark city flashed into her mind again. When she dreamed about it she felt as if she was coming home. She didn't understand how the city worked, how the strange vibrant colours shone out in the darkness the way they did, or how there could be no stars in the sky. But she knew her way around. If she kept walking she would reach a dark square before a dark castle, and there would be a statue there, surrounded by flowers that glowed from within.

Bianca yearned for it. Somehow, she promised herself fiercely, she would find a way into the streets she walked in her dreams. She would get to that dark city, and uncover its secrets. There would be no rest for her until she did.

Don't miss the next thrilling book in
THE LAST APPRENTICE series –
Coming soon . . .

Now that she's saved her city, Bianca has risen in the
ranks to become court painter to the Countess
Catriona. But all is not well. Court life is duller than
she would have expected, her old friends are angry
and jealous, and Bianca can't stop dreaming about
the dark city she glimpsed during the Baron's escape.

When she finds a way to cross into the dark city,
Bianca discovers a strange new world – and begins
to unearth secrets of her own hidden past. Danger
lurks in both cities, and no one believes Bianca's
warnings. With her loyalties tested on both sides,
Bianca wonders if she is on the side of good, or
evil . . .